ANGELS AND DONKEYS

Happy 3rd
birthday Bngt

To enjoy the
history, know Bundel
heard Nelly Trocmé
Hewitt speak in
DC

To know we learned
of Trocme's in our
Peace Studies / Colman
McCarthy curriculum

Love Mom + Dad
2001

ANGELS AND DONKEYS

Tales for Christmas and Other Times

ANDRÉ TROCMÉ

Translated by NELLY TROCMÉ HEWETT

Good Books

Intercourse, PA 17534
800/762-7171
www.goodbks.com

Biblical citations are from the HOLY BIBLE: THE NEW INTERNATIONAL
VERSION, © 1973, 1978, 1984 by the International Bible Society, used
by permission of Zondervan Bible Publishers.

Cover design by Cheryl Benner
Design by Dawn J. Ranck

ANGELS AND DONKEYS: TALES FOR CHRISTMAS AND OTHER TIMES
Copyright © 1998 by Good Books, Intercourse, PA 17534
International Standard Book Number: 1-56148-263-3
Library of Congress Catalog Card Number: 98-42121

A version of these stories was first published in French.

Library of Congress Cataloging-in-Publication Data
Trocmé, André, 1901-1971.
    [Des anges et des ânes. English]
    Angels and donkeys : tales for Christmas and other times /
André Trocmé ; translated by Nelly Trocmé Hewett.
    p. cm.
    Summary: A collection of tales, many based on stories from
the Bible, told by the author, a French minister, around the huge
Christmas tree in the church in Le Chambon sur Lignon.
    ISBN: 1-56148-263-3
    1. Jesus Christ--Juvenile fiction. 2. Children's stories,
French--Translations into English. [1. Jesus Christ--Fiction.
2. Christian life--Fiction. 3. Christmas--Fiction. 4. Short stories.]
I. Trocmé Hewett, Nelly. II. Title.
PZ7.T7395An 1998
[Fic]--dc21   98-42121
                                                       CIP
                                                       AC

Table of Contents

A portion of the royalties from the sale of this book will be donated to The Fellowship of Reconciliation.

Before You Read These Stories . . .

The stories in this collection were told to the children of Le Chambon-sur-Lignon while France was under siege, occupied by Hitler's troops. The people of the area had formed an underground network for saving refugees, many of them Jewish children.

The rescuers did not know what their neighbors were doing. No one talked. Where did these people get their courage to risk their lives to save strangers? (The people of the Plateau are credited with helping nearly 5,000 refugees, about 3,500 of them Jewish, many of whom are still alive today.)

The stories in this book are part of that story. For the courage to do what one knows one should do is very often sparked by the memory of a story.

These original stories were told by Pastor André Trocmé by the huge lighted tree on Christmas day in the Protestant (Huguenot) church in that small mountain village, during the poverty and anxiety of

1

wartime uncertainty. Everyone knew that death and betrayal surrounded them on every side. Many of the themes in the stories are couched references to the courage one needs in such circumstances. This marks the first appearance of these stories in English.

In the U.S. Holocaust Memorial Museum in Washington, D.C. is a room dedicated to Rescuers. There a display features a tribute to the courage of the people of the Plateau Vivarais-Lignon and their leaders, among them the Trocmé family, Pastor Theis, and Daniel Trocmé, who died in the concentration camp. Included in the exhibit is a picture of Pastor André Trocmé and his young family.

To honor the memories of André and Magda Trocmé, half of all royalties earned by sales of this book will be donated to the International Fellowship of Reconciliation. The Fellowship is an international and nondenominational organization concerned with peace and the nonviolent resolution of conflicts.

An Introduction

Each one of the stories in this small book was written to be told during a Christmas celebration for children. The author himself told the stories, standing next to the traditional tree.

May the reader remember that several of these stories were written during the occupation of France by Hitler, and that the gospel of the birth, the death, and the resurrection of Christ was the only valid answer to the diabolical horrors perpetrated by the princes of this world.

Why angels? Because the Christmas skies are filled with messengers delivering the good news of the Prince of Peace's coming.

As for the little donkeys of the New Testament, they are closer to angels than to people who are strong, powerful, and intelligent.

—André Trocmé

3

I Remember Christmas in Le Chambon

High on a plateau in the mountains of central France, Christmas was a magic time for the children of my village, Le Chambon-sur-Lignon.

In the 1930s and 1940s, the daily routine of life did not spoil us, for beggars came to the door asking for food, and rumblings of war haunted us constantly. Hand-me-down clothes, often mended and patched, were our lot, and a secondhand sled or a rickety old bicycle represented the greatest of gifts.

But to us the children, life was full of wonder anyway. Caught in the rhythm of school and play, we believed that every changing season brought joy—spring, with its fields of wild daffodils (we called them "*barbelottes*") as far as the eye could see; summer, which revealed who was courageous enough to swim in the very cold Lignon (our small mountain river), and who was fast enough to pick pint after pint of wild blueberries and still eat plenty of them; fall, with its warm colors suddenly ripped away by wild rains; and finally winter, with its chilly winds (*la burle*) sweeping horizontally over the plateau, chasing snow around the corners of our granite homes and farms, piling it up in elegant curved ridges (*les congères*) as high as our parents were tall! Dotted with thick forests of pine trees, the countryside turned into a severe and mysterious panorama in black and white.

"How bleak!" you might exclaim. But we the children didn't care, for the coming of winter meant Christmas and its magic.

The old Huguenot church belonged to the countryside. Built of hand-cut granite blocks, it was plain and massive. It had a simple facade with a window on both sides of wide double doors. On the lintel were carved the words, "Love one another." (*"Aimez-vous les uns les autres."*) And on the top of the single gable stood an open steeple sheltering a heavy, brass bell.

The wide double doors opened into an aisle lined on both sides with very straight and hard wooden benches, and with two rows of tall columns, all alike and yet a bit different: each one had been hand-hewn from the straight shaft of a tall fir tree. A slightly raised platform closed the very end of the aisle. Above it on the far wall hung the preacher's pulpit, high enough to tower over the assembly. Painted on the wall to the left of the pulpit stood the words, "The master is here." (*"Le Maître est ici."*) And on the right side, "He is calling you." (*"Il t'appelle."*)

No frills, no microphone, no stained glass windows or carpet runners, no organ. For heat— two large iron stoves that turned red hot when they were well stocked with wood.

You might still wonder, "How could such a dismal place be filled with magic on Christmas day?" Well, ask the children of that time who are now grandfathers and grandmothers. They will assure you that it *did* turn magic.

I remember one Christmas in particular. It was very cold and the snow was deep. The double doors had been thrown wide open and the benches pushed aside. Into the church came a draw horse, a real one, puffing little clouds of warm breath through its large nostrils into the cold air. The horse was dragging a giant balsam tree, cut two hours before in the forest. The horse walked all the way up the aisle where the trunk of the tree could rest on the platform. The church elders had removed a stone slab in the floor in order to accommodate the tree. They did the same thing year after year, knowing exactly how to erect it securely and decorate it.

On the afternoon of December 25th, when we children heard the church bell ring, we ran down the village streets as fast as we could, anxious not to be one minute late, our galoshes (*sabots*) ringing on the ice.

Our Sunday School teachers assigned each of us to a designated seating area. And that's when *the magic began*. A hundred candles covered the tree, real live candles welcoming us with their shimmering lights. It looked like a thousand or more candles with all the tinsel hanging on the branches.

Led by the enthusiastic voices of Pastors Theis and Trocmé, we sang many Christmas songs accompanied by an old puffing reed organ. Someone read the Christmas story, and we knew it so well we could anticipate every word of it.

All the children received brown paper bags labeled with their names. Each bag contained an orange and a tangerine, some dates and candies, some nuts and raisins and a small gift. But the most amazing of all were the two or three (*papillottes*) in each—candies wrapped distinctively, each with a tiny firecracker taped to the inside of its paper. If one pulled the two end tabs, a cap hidden in the center would explode with a loud "pow!" These, of course, were not to be enjoyed in the church. They were for later.

Finally came the best part of our Christmas celebration—a special Christmas story written by Pastor André Trocmé. Beside him, his friend Roger Darcissac had set up a large white screen where Chinese lantern pictures moved progressively to illustrate the story.

Pastor Trocmé—my father—told a new story each year. He was tall and slim, with intense blue eyes looking at each one of us through his old-fashioned, round glasses. Carried away by the joy of the children and the fun of the story, he paced back and forth in front of the tree, acting and gesturing. Sometimes he was serious; at other times he laughed at his own stories, spontaneously adding details that surprised him and amused us to no end.

The *magic* was everywhere. Our mouths stood open, and we were captivated, swept from reality into another world that had nothing to do with our village, a world where things always ended up the right way, a world which was hard to leave behind when the story came to an end.

Angels and Donkeys is a collection of many of these Christmas stories.

I dedicate this book to the children of the world who know very well that when it comes to goodness and peace, donkeys and angels are often much smarter than grown-ups.

—Nelly Trocmé Hewett

The Rich Man and the Poor Man

a story about strangers

Under the reign of Caesar Augustus, at the time when Quirinius was the governor of Syria, two men lived in Bethlehem, a town in Judea.

The first man was immensely rich, and the second was very poor.

The rich one dressed in fine linen. He lived in a big house surrounded with granaries and stables in which he accumulated his belongings: herds of cattle and sheep and large harvests of wheat, musk, and oil.

This man came from the family line of King David, and he had the greatest respect from his neighbors because of his royal origins.

So, on a Sabbath day, the rich man went to the synagogue. He walked through the congregation, up to the first place in front where he sat. The reader opened the book of the Prophet Isaiah and read from Chapter 55:

"Give ear, and come to me; hear me that your soul may live. I will make an everlasting covenant with you, my unfailing kindnesses promised to David. See, I have made him a witness to the peoples, a leader and commander of the peoples."

Once back home, the rich man remembered those words and felt an enormous pride from them, for he did not doubt he would be called to great glory on the day when the Messiah, his relative, would return to the throne of David.

The poor man dressed in a crude material

woven from goat hair. He lived in a little house, the last one at the edge of town. It had only one room which he shared with an ox and a donkey, his only possessions.

On the very same Sabbath day, this man also went to the synagogue, but he was so poorly dressed that he stood by the door, at the last place. He listened to the reading of Isaiah's text; he rejoiced because of God's promises. And as the reader read on he heard the words that follow in chapter 58:

"Is it not to share your food with the hungry and to provide the poor wanderer with shelter—"

Once back home, the poor man meditated over the words he had heard and resolved to put them into practice.

In those times, following Caesar's orders, a census of the whole earth's population was taken. Everyone went to register, each in his hometown.

The descendants of families originally from Bethlehem flocked into the village, and among them came those from the family of King David.

The rich man had his house wide open, welcoming all strangers. Among them, he hoped to discover the King of Israel who would lead him to glory. And since he was a shrewd businessman, he did not forget to have his guests pay a high price for board and room.

As for the poor man, he recalled the words of the Prophet Isaiah, and he would have liked to welcome strangers. But no one wanted to come under his roof, so repulsed were they at the thought of sleeping on straw, next to an ox and a donkey.

One evening, a man and a woman came into the village and asked where they could spend the night. Since there was no room left anywhere, someone directed them to the rich man's house. The rich man greeted them at the door and asked whether they had any money.

"No," they answered. "We come from Nazareth, in Galilee. We are modest people, without money."

So the rich man closed the door, shouting at them, "Don't bother me anymore! My house is full. I can't take you in."

Thrown out by all the inhabitants of Bethlehem, the man and the woman arrived at the poor man's house. The latter was so happy to welcome them, he invited them in, washed their feet, gave them something to eat, and prepared a straw bed for his guests.

And that same night, these people had a baby. Since there was no cradle in the house, his mother wrapped the infant and put him to sleep in a manger.

A few days later, three new travelers arrived in Bethlehem. They spoke a foreign language and inquired about a newly born king. They were directed to the rich man's house which was brilliantly lit and overlooked the town. They immediately knocked at the door.

The rich man came to open the door, and when he saw the three wise men dressed in splendid garments and escorted by a large staff, he had no doubt that descendants of

King David stood in front of him. He let them in, welcomed them with all the traditional honors, had his slaves wash their feet, anointed their heads with oil, kissed them, and had a grand supper prepared for them.

However, one of the travelers spoke up and asked, "Where is the King of the Jews who was just born? For we saw his star in the Orient and we came to adore him."

The rich man did not know what to answer.

So the three kings stood up and left. They scoured all the streets of Bethlehem, knocked on all the doors, receiving everywhere the same answer, "We don't know whom you are speaking about."

They finally came to the very last house, yet they hesitated to knock on the door because it looked so miserable. The poor man opened the door. A feeble light shone inside. The kings asked, "Where is the King of the Jews who was just born?"

The poor man answered, "I don't have a king nor the son of a king at my house. All I have

ANGELS AND DONKEYS

are poor people who came from Nazareth in Galilee, and their little child is asleep in a manger."

Disappointed, the kings were about to leave when they noticed that the bright star had stopped above the house. They were overwhelmed by a great joy, for then they knew they had reached the end of their journey.

They entered the house and saw the child with Mary his mother. They bowed in front of him and worshiped him. They opened their treasures, offering gifts of gold, incense, and myrrh.

Because of them, the poor man learned he had given hospitality to the son of God who takes away the sin of the world. Falling to his knees, he shed abundant tears, so grateful was his heart for the honor of sheltering the Son of God.

When the rich man learned what had happened, he exploded with great anger and immediately sent emissaries to King Herod to accuse the newborn child.

The Old Woman and Her Stove

a story about being willing
to sacrifice everything,
even risking one's life,
to warm the child

Not so many years ago, somewhere in northern France, lived a poor old woman. Her only furniture was a big wooden bed, an armoire or freestanding closet, and, most importantly, a Flemish stove.

The poor woman didn't have all her mind anymore. Her memory had left her, along with the members of her family who had died one after the other. She believed that she had transformed her stove into a real person who kept her company. Other people look for the companionship of dogs, of cats, or of birds. This woman loved her stove; we must understand her and forgive her.

It is true that this stove with its flat hat, its two arms, and its small round mouth resembled a malicious, little, dark goblin. She brushed it and polished it, and she spent all her money to feed it pretty coal pieces. She paid a great deal for the pleasure of seeing her stove happy. And happiness made it roar! Its cheeks would turn red! The old woman's cheeks would turn pink. She encouraged her fine companion, "There, you're happy. You don't have anything to complain about. Ah, I will spoil you, you'll see!"

Unfortunately, things didn't always go so well. Some days the wind sent the draft down the chimney, and the stove billowed out big puffs of smoke like a grumbling and impolite

ANGELS AND DONKEYS

fellow. Then the old woman became angry, brandishing her poker and scolding her stove, "So that's the way you thank me! I won't give you anything anymore if you are not polite! Ah, today's stoves are not as they used to be!"

The months went by, and, thanks to her stove, the old woman survived the foggy winters of her humid homeland. However, one day shortly before Christmas, something came to interrupt the monotony of the old woman's life.

She was invited to a meeting at her neighbor's house. A minister spoke. (The old woman had no idea what a "minister" was.) She found the hymns quite pretty and declared that the gentleman had spoken well. But she did not tell anyone how the message she heard had plunged her into a deep ferment. Old people tell each other a lot of stories, especially about past and present miseries. They shake their heads, they sigh and wipe a tear. But never had a story upset her so much. A child, she was told, had been born on straw in a place called Bethlehem, and his father and mother, Mr. Joseph and Mrs. Mary, did not even have enough to cover the baby and keep it warm!

Between you and me, she was indignant that the gentleman at the meeting and all those well dressed people didn't think of collecting some money to send to those poor people. Jostling her stove, she confided in it.

She slept very poorly that night. She was one of those simple souls who suffers more because of the misery of others than because of her own. In her mind, a plan took shape.

At first confused, it soon became clear and commanding. Oh, it didn't take shape without some inner fighting. It is never without a struggle that a person gets rid of her most precious possession. The widow of the Bible certainly had a long inner quarrel before dropping her coin in the poor box inside the Temple of Jerusalem.

By the next day on Christmas Eve she had

made up her mind. Some old people are private, and they don't like to tell their stories to others who are indiscreet.

So she did not tell anyone about her sacrifice. She polished her stove and then summoned a railroad employee whom she knew. The employee was as ill-informed about religion as she was and addressed a box as she dictated: "Mr. Joseph, in Bethlehem." Then he took her stove to the station, thinking that after the holidays he'd find the best way to send the package to its destination.

The old woman paid the shipping costs and, without a tear, without uneasiness, watched her companion leave the house. She was completely absorbed by her dream: she had to stop the child in Bethlehem from being cold.

The day went by, in solitude. No one came to visit her. Toward evening she noticed she was shivering, and she could not get warm even in bed. Outside, an ice-cold wind started to blow and snow fell.

The old woman sank into an agitated sleep. In her dream she painstakingly attempted to clear a path through the wind and the snow, trying to reach the child. But she never could get to the baby. She grew immensely fatigued so that she could not go forward anymore. She was burning hot and yet shivering from exhaustion and cold.

And then suddenly, everything calmed down. She felt immersed in a great light. She felt well. She realized that she had reached her goal. The child would not be cold anymore.

The next morning on Christmas day, the neighbor woman was sweeping the snow off her front steps when she discovered that the old woman's door was wide open. Curious, she entered the kitchen. The wind had pushed open the door, and snow had piled up in the house deprived of fire. It formed a long ridge leading up to the bed.

The old woman had died. She was resting

in her bed, ice-cold, her calm features reflecting happiness.

A few days later, the railroad employee found the broken pieces of a rusty stove in a corner. He wondered with astonishment what had happened to the shiny object he had so carefully transported to the station. For the old stove had died at the same time as its owner, having warmed the child in the old woman's dream, the mission with which she had entrusted it.

Nicodemus

a story about giving,
kindness to strangers,
and the humble and the poor

"Rabbi Gamaliel! Rabbi Gamaliel!"
A voice woke Rabbi Gamaliel who had just retired for the night. He got up and opened the door.

"Rabbi Gamaliel," a woman was calling insistently, "come quickly to my house! I think my husband Nicodemus has gone crazy! He keeps singing and crying, repeating always the same thing: 'My eyes have seen the king!' Or: 'All I had was my poverty!'"

"Don't stay outside," answered Gamaliel. "Come in and tell me everything."

And this is the story Nicodemus' wife told Gamaliel.

You know, Rabbi Gamaliel, that in spite of his young age—only 30—Nicodemus is considered to be one of the doctors, in fact, the most capable of explaining ancient prophecies.

So, the day before yesterday, King Herod called him to the palace for a consultation. Nicodemus' colleagues from the main synagogue were also invited.

The King asked, "According to the scriptures, tell me where Christ is supposed to be born."

"In Bethlehem, in Judea," the doctors answered unanimously.

It happened that the three Wise Men were standing next to Herod's throne. They had helped originate this consultation and they exclaimed, "Let's go to Bethlehem, for we want to give homage to the King of the Jews who was just born. We saw his star in the Orient."

My husband was very agitated when he returned from Herod's palace. Yesterday he woke me very early. "Woman," said he, "prepare the beautiful white wool coat you wove with your own hands, and have my little gray donkey saddled."

Then he put 30 silver pieces—our whole fortune—into his money bag. "I also must give homage to the newborn king," said he. And he left for Bethlehem, without forgetting his sword should he encounter some bandits.

Oh, Rabbi Gamaliel! Tonight, Nicodemus came home without his sword; he does not have the beautiful white coat I wove for him; he lost his gray donkey; his money purse containing 30 silver pieces, our total fortune, has disappeared; he shivers in his light linen tunic which is dirty and dusty, the only garment he has left. But he keeps on singing. I think he's crazy!"

Rabbi Gamaliel went to Nicodemus' house and found him in the state of exaltation his wife had described, pacing back and forth.

"Sit down a minute," said the rabbi, "and tell me everything that happened in the right order."

"Well, said Nicodemus, "yesterday morning I left Jerusalem through the so-called Manure Gate, located near the shanties of the poor whose job is to sort garbage. A beggar, squatting on the edge of the path, stopped me, saying, 'My good sir, give me your coat. I am cold.' He was shivering in the early morning air. And I answered, 'I cannot give you my beautiful white woolen coat, woven by my wife. Besides, I have an important mission to fulfill. I am going to Bethlehem to greet the newly born Messiah. I don't have time to waste with you.'

"But as I was about to go on my way, the words of the ancient prophet came to my mind: 'If you see a naked man, cover him.' How could I even appear in front of the

ANGELS AND DONKEYS

Messiah if I disobeyed such a commandment? And before even taking time to think, I had given the beggar the beautiful white woolen coat woven by my wife's hands. Then I proceeded to Bethlehem.

"As I came close to the En Roguel Fountain, a robber surged in front of me and grabbed the bridle of my donkey. 'Give me your money,' said he. 'I would gladly do so,' said I, 'but I am going to Bethlehem to give it as a gift to the newly born King of the Jews. Don't you believe in the King of the Jews who must free Israel?'

"'Of course I do,' he answered. 'It is to prepare for his coming that I am hiding in the bushes. But you, Pharisee, you're telling me stories to escape from me. Give me your money, and quickly!'

"I could have attempted to go by him, hitting him with my sword, but Isaiah's words came to my mind: '. . . to us a son is given . . . and he will be called Prince of Peace.' Should I commit a murder in order to celebrate the birth of the

Prince of Peace? So I willingly gave the robber my purse containing all our fortune, and my sword, now useless. And I continued on my way to Bethlehem.

"As my little donkey kept trotting happily— I could already see Bethlehem in the distance—I was called upon by a man walking laboriously along the road. 'Lord,' said he in a foreign accent, 'I came from Damas and am heading for Alexandria in Egypt. My dying father has called me to his side. Alas, the stones of the road wounded my feet which now refuse to carry me any further. Lend me your gray donkey. I'll give it back to you on my way home.'

"'I also have an important mission to accomplish,' I answered. 'I am going to Bethlehem to celebrate the birth of the newly born Savior of the Jews.'

"'The Savior of the Jews is not my concern since I am a stranger,' replied the man. 'Besides, Bethlehem is so close, and Egypt is so far. . .'

ANGELS AND DONKEYS

"I was about to go on my way when the words of the Psalm came back to my mind. 'I was young and now I am old, yet I have never seen the righteous forsaken . . . They are always generous and lend freely . . .'

"'Well, take my gray donkey,' I told the stranger. 'I am Rabbi Nicodemus from Jerusalem. Bring it back to me as soon as possible.'

"Thus I arrived in Bethlehem, totally stripped of my possessions, dressed only with a simple linen tunic."

"Did you find the Messiah?" interrupted Rabbi Gamaliel eagerly.

"Not immediately, Rabbi Gamaliel, not right away! Because I first had to go through the apprenticeship of poverty.

"My first visit was to the Chief of the Synagogue. I asked him, 'Where is the new-born Messiah?'

"When he saw my miserable outfit, he refused to believe I was Rabbi Nicodemus

Nicodemus   31

from Jerusalem. He took me for a wicked joker and showed me the door.

"I went to see all the leading citizens of Bethlehem, one after the other, but no one took me seriously. They mocked me, threatened me, and chased me away. Although the law forbids us to have contacts with lowlife people, I nevertheless called on the toll-gatherer. But even he treated me with scorn.

"As night was falling, I knocked on the door of a local inn. 'Please take me in for one night only,' I asked of the innkeeper. 'I'll pay you later.'

"'An honest man doesn't travel without luggage and money,' he replied. 'Get on your way!' And he released his dogs after me.

"I was resigning myself to sleeping on the street when a man walked by me. Because of his strong smell, I knew he was one of those shepherds who sleep in the stable with their sheep.

"'Good fellow,' said I in a beseeching voice, 'could you give me a piece of bread and some shelter for the night? A bale of straw would be enough.'

"'Certainly,' answered the man in his warm peasant voice. 'But not before you accompany me to the stable where a little child born the day before yesterday is sleeping. Every night we take food to his parents who are poor Galileans without money. They came for the census. Besides, angels appeared to us during the night, convincing us that this child was the Messiah. They said, "You will find a swaddled child laying in a manger; that is how you will recognize him."'"

At this point, Nicodemus was seized by deep emotion. To Rabbi Gamaliel's astonishment, he started again to pace back and forth, repeating, "I saw the King and all I had was my poverty."

Gamaliel interrupted him somewhat impatiently. "Tell me, how was the King, Nicodemus?"

"Listen to me, Rabbi Gamaliel. If I had entered the stable with my sword, dressed in the beautiful white coat woven by my wife, my money purse bulging with 30 silver coins, and riding on my grey donkey, I would not have been able to believe that the child of poor people was really the Son of God. But because the shepherds accepted me as one of them, because they moved over to make a bit of room for me, because Joseph and Mary from Nazareth welcomed me with kindness, I understood that God did not choose the wise or the intelligent, the rich or the powerful, to manifest himself to the people of Israel. God chose the illiterate and the humble, the poor and the weak. Can you understand that, Rabbi Gamaliel? I fear you might not!"

"Tomorrow morning, I will go back with you to Bethlehem," said Gamaliel. "Go and rest. It is getting late."

Early the next morning, the two men started off. They were not prepared for the three astonishing encounters they would make on the way. Sure enough, no sooner had they passed through the Manure Gate than a man ran toward them.

"Rabbi," he exclaimed when he saw Nicodemus, "I am so happy to have found you again!"

"But . . .what have you done with the beautiful white coat I gave you?" asked Nicodemus.

"I gave it to the Messiah, just born in Bethlehem," exclaimed the man.

"How so? Did you go to Bethlehem?"

"Yes, my Lord. I first tried to sell your coat since, as a professional beggar, I have established a business with the items given me. But your goodness moved me so that I left to look for you so I could return your coat to you. Once in Bethlehem, a shepherd showed me the stable where you had slept, and there I found a man, a woman, and a little child much poorer than myself. Before even thinking, I had given them the coat. And as I was making this gift, my eyes were opened, and I understood that the child on whose feet I had spread the coat was indeed the Messiah you had talked about. I hastily ran back to give you the good news."

"We are returning to Bethlehem to enter the service of the Messiah. Come along with us." And the man followed them.

It is near the fountain of En Roguel that the three travelers made their second encounter. A man threw himself at Nicodemus' feet.

"Lord," said he, "forgive me."

"Get up," Nicodemus told him with kindness. "I forgive you since you are repenting. You want to give my money back to me?"

"Alas, no, my Lord. I can't return it. I gave it away. Take me to a judge if you want, but first of all listen to my adventure. When I opened your purse the other morning, I discovered I had become rich. I immediately decided to abandon my life of robbery and flee to Egypt.

So I went to Bethlehem, bought nice clothes, and went to the inn where I was welcomed with great honors because of my money.

"As I dined with three Wise Men from the Orient, they told me a marvelous story. They had seen a star in the sky that showed them the way to Bethlehem, and the previous night, in a stable, they had found the King of the Jews who must free Israel.

"So I told myself, it is indeed true what the Pharisee told me, though I thought it was a fairy tale.

"I immediately went to the stable where things were exactly as described by the Wise Men. But the gifts they brought made me smile: incense, myrrh in a golden ornamental box! If the poor Galileans ever tried to sell these items, they would be accused of stealing them!

"But before giving it a moment of reflection, I had poured on the infant's mother's lap what was left of the money I had stolen from you, a real fortune indeed!

As I did this, my eyes were opened, and I understood this small child was the Son of David, the King of the Jews I was waiting for. I immediately started to look for you to tell you the good news and ask for your forgiveness."

"You are forgiven," said Nicodemus. "Come with us to Bethlehem to enter the service of the newborn child."

And the man followed.

Filled with joy, the four men came within sight of Bethlehem. They witnessed a frightening spectacle: acrid smoke rose above the town, and one could hear cries and wails like those uttered by women near a dead body. Night was falling as the travelers entered the town. A woman fled past them, holding a little dead child on her bosom. "Herod's soldiers killed my son," she said, crying.

A shepherd they met on the square described the catastrophe. "We were in the fields when we heard some shouting, but we arrived too late. Soldiers had forced their way into homes and massacred all the boys under two years of age, fearing that the King of the Jews might escape. For the Wise Men had imprudently mentioned him to Herod, the old bloodthirsty madman who kills without pity all pretenders to the throne of Israel. Come and see what's left of the stable."

Only smoking ruins were visible on the spot where the stable once stood. Hoping to find the remains of the little King of the Jews and to bury them, the shepherds, in tears, were moving aside burning stones with their bare hands. Nicodemus and his friends started helping them when, in the darkness, a hand touched his shoulder.

"Is it you?" said a foreign voice which he immediately recognized. "Is it really you who lent me your donkey the day before yesterday?"

"Yes," answered Nicodemus.

"Stop searching among the dead for the one who is still alive," continued the man. "I was looking for shelter last night and was welcomed by Joseph and Mary. Your little gray donkey and I spent the night in this stable. In the early dawn, divinely warned by a dream, Joseph took the child and his mother and left for Egypt before the arrival of Herod's soldiers."

"What can we hope from their flight?" interrupted Nicodemus. "Aren't they going to die from cold and poverty in the desert?"

"They won't die," answered the man, "for the child was wrapped in a large coat of handwoven wool. His father carried on his belt a purse of silver coins, and his mother rode away on your little gray donkey, which I gave them so that the stones of the road would not wound Mary's feet."

"But I thought the Savior of the Jews did not interest foreigners," stated Nicodemus."

"So it was," said the stranger, "but at the very moment when I gave away your donkey,

ANGELS AND DONKEYS

my eyes were opened, and I understood the little child was not only the King of the Jews, but also the Savior of all people."

One night many years later, an important rabbi, one of the best known doctors of the law in Jerusalem, went to consult a poor carpenter from Nazareth who happened through town. The great scholar was trying to locate the Messiah whose trail he had lost for 30 years. His colleagues mocked him for his obsession in looking among the poor and the ignorant.

"Teacher," asked the scholar with humility, "I know you are a learned man who came from God. What should one do to see the Kingdom of God?"

Jesus answered, "You must be born again; you must start your life again in total poverty, as if you didn't know anything."

Nicodemus understood he had reached the end of his long search and that he had found the child born in Bethlehem.

Hospitality

a story about the temptations
of those who say they want to help others
and the way true hospitality multiplies

Long ago, when Archelaus was King of
Judea and Samaria, there was a town
inhabited only by Samaritans. It was the most
forbidding of all the Samaritan towns. Sad,
blackish, and built with volcanic stones, it
kept watch at the entrance of a narrow gorge.
The Jewish travelers going from Judea to
Galilee had to go through that gorge and
were forced to pay heavy tolls.

As they came through the village, travelers

quickened their steps to avoid the insulting remarks of the people and the stones thrown at them by the street boys. They planned their trip so as to cross the village in the middle of the day, for as soon as night came, the population locked all the city gates tightly, abandoning the travelers to the terrors of an arid countryside infested by jackals.

A small distance away from the village lived an old woman, all alone in a hovel. She was poor and nasty.

She hated men, since her long dead husband used to beat her. She hated women because some had slandered her and at one time envied her. She hated children because she never had a child of her own. All she had to survive was a goat, a woolen mantle, a cheese, and a piece of bread.

It happened that one evening a man and a woman knocked on her door. The town gates had already been closed. The couple was obviously very tired. They were Jews.

"What do you want?" asked the old woman

in a harsh voice through her barely opened door.

"Have pity on us," said the man, with the look of people who are being hunted. "The police of Archelaus are looking for us. King Herod, Archelaus' father tried to kill our child in Bethlehem. We fled to Egypt. There we learned that Herod had died and so we started on our way back. But Archelaus is even more cruel than his father. He just massacred 3000 people in Jerusalem, and his men almost arrested us in Bethlehem. We want to leave this cursed kingdom and go to Galilee."

The old woman observed them spitefully. As a Samaritan, she hated Jews.

"Get on your way, you cursed Jews," said she. "If the police are after you, you have no doubt committed a crime. I don't like to get in trouble with the King's officers."

"Have pity on us!" cried the woman. "We are lost; I am afraid; I am weary."

The old woman sneered. "And who do you

think I am? A millionaire, maybe? I am even poorer than you. No one comes to my help. A crumbling hovel for shelter, a goat that gives a bit of milk—these are my total belongings, and yet you want me to share with you?" As she spoke, she started closing the door.

But at that very moment the traveler opened her cloak slightly, and, in the curve of her arm, the old woman noticed something beautiful—a tiny infant quietly asleep. There followed a moment of silence, an almost supernatural silence. Then suddenly, the old woman opened the door.

"Come in!" she growled.

Settled by the fire, the man started complaining again. "I'm hungry," he said. "We were so scared we didn't even take time to eat."

The old woman stood up and fetched her cheese and bread from the closet. "All I have left," she hissed, throwing the few pieces she found on the table. The man seized the little bit of food and shared it with his wife.

Then it was his wife who started to complain. She was shivering as if she had a fever. "I'm cold," she moaned.

Without a word, the old woman took off the hook an old mantle woven in rough wool. She put it on the young mother's shoulders. With a smile, the traveler accepted the gift, like a queen receiving homage.

And then it was the baby's turn. Hidden in the folds of his mother's arms, he started to cry.

"He is thirsty," his mother murmured.

Still moved by the same invisible force, the old woman kneeled in the darkest corner of the room and started milking the goat.

"How lucky to own a goat!" sighed the traveler. "I have no more milk for my little one. Ah, if only I could buy a goat. . . but we are too poor to do so."

The old woman stood up straight and furious. The bowl full of milk shook in her hand. "That's the limit," she shouted. "You took my food, you took my cloak, and now you also want my goat! You impudent and invading Jews, as long as you are here, you might as well take my little house and kick me out."

At once the mother uncovered the baby to give him a drink. The baby seemed consoled, smiling as he watched the fire.

The old woman gazed on him. "Take my goat," she sighed. "It will be for him."

The next morning the travelers started on their way, taking along the cloak and the goat. They didn't know how to thank the old woman. She watched them go and then stretched out on her straw litter, ready to die there. Never had she been so content. She was living the joy of those who give everything away and feel marvelously free with regard to worldly possessions.

The man and the woman also smiled joyfully as they prepared to cross through the town. They paid their toll fee. Everything seemed to go without troubles when a fat man stopped them with a shout. It was the village butcher.

"Hey, you there, what is this animal you're taking with you? I think I recognize it. I'm the one who sold it to the old woman!"

"It was given to us!" answered the stranger.

"Given to you?" said the butcher in his biggest voice. "What a fib! This animal belongs to the poorest woman in the village. You thieves. You preying Jews who always take what doesn't belong to you!"

A crowd was gathering, and another voice was heard. A long and skinny man was speaking, the weaver of the village.

"And this cloak. Didn't you steal it also? It belongs to the old woman. I recognize it. I am the one who wove it."

"You would also have taken her house, had you been able to do so," hissed a small hunchback. "I rent it to her!" This man was the usurer, the owner of most of the town's houses.

"What should we do with these people,

teacher?" asked the usurer of an important official dressed in white.

"Let them be stoned," ordered the official. And already the crowd was picking up stones.

At that, the stranger opened her cloak and showed the child asleep in her arms. He was so beautiful, so peaceful; he slept so deeply in the middle of all that noise that the Samaritan crowd, dumbfounded, backed away. Their wry expressions turned into slight smiles. Their hands relaxed, dropping the stones.

"Let them go," said the teacher.

The night that followed these events turned out to be a sleepless one for several inhabitants of the Samaritan village.

The butcher could not keep the old woman out of his mind since she was now deprived of her only goat. Strangely enough, as he thought of the two strangers who had deprived her of her animal, he didn't feel any anger. On the contrary, he was the one who felt guilty. He reviewed in his mind the many hundreds of animals that belonged to him, and he began to feel responsible for the many injustices done to the old woman.

The weaver was thinking about the woman's cloak. Meanwhile, he had dozens of other cloaks stashed in his chests. He also felt a touch of remorse.

The usurer kept turning one way and then the other on his bed, ashamed for having dared to ask for rent when the roof of the old lady's hovel was full of holes.

And the teacher, who thought he was in the clear with God since he regularly gave the church one-tenth of his income, was now suffering morally. He was thinking of all the cheeses and barrels full of flour lined up in his cellar.

The next morning, the four men met at the door of the poor woman, as if they had actually made plans to meet there! The woman, so weakened by lack of food, could hardly open the door for them.

"Woman," said the butcher, "here are the two most beautiful goats from my herd to replace the one that was stolen from you."

"Here are the two most handsome cloaks from my chests," said the weaver. "Now you can cover yourself since your own cloak was taken."

"Nothing was taken from me," said the old woman to the astonished men. "I am the one who gave away everything, and my cheese and bread as well. I am going to die and I am quite happy about it."

"You won't die," replied the teacher. "Here are two cheeses and two jugs filled with flour. And when you have nothing left, I'll bring you more."

"Teacher, you won't have the trouble of coming out this far," interrupted the usurer. "This hovel is too far from the village and too run-down. From today on, the old woman can live for free in a building I have at the end of my garden."

ANGELS AND DONKEYS

From the moment when the old woman passed through the gates, everything changed in the Samaritan town. She brought a freedom about owning things and a feeling of generosity that spread throughout the whole population. The people who had once been so intent on making money learned to help each other and found great pleasure in making gifts. The council of Elders decided not to close the village gates at night. They canceled all toll fees; in fact, they opened an inn where all travelers could lodge, free of charge.

The townspeople whitewashed their village, and soon it had the reputation of being the most welcoming village in the whole of Samaria.

Legend has it—although I am unable to verify it—that that same year, in the village, a little child was born. Later he came to be known as the Good Samaritan.

How Donkeys Got the Spirit of Contradiction

*a story about saving children,
and the courage it takes
to go against social convention
and expectations*

Until the birth of Jesus, donkeys were like anyone else; that is, just like human beings. I mean just like *grown-up* human beings, not like children. Children have always had the Spirit of Contradiction. But donkeys used to be docile, just like grown-ups today.

Here is how things changed.

In Bethlehem, at the entrance of the town, lived a Samaritan. He was a good man. He tried as much as possible to help people forget he was a Samaritan. He thought, spoke, and dressed just like anyone else. He was a conformist.

Everyone respects social conventions. Each of us likes to welcome our guests into clean, well decorated homes. Our Samaritan, who was single and whose house was in disarray, preferred to receive no one. There was one exception—if his best friend warned him way ahead of time, he would allow him to come into his house.

Everyone belongs to a clique. We trust the members of our families and our intimate friends. We like to do them favors. But of strangers, *Everyone* has distrust. We don't know whom we are dealing with.

So thought our Samaritan also.

Everyone is scared of traveling alone in deserted areas in the evening when roads are especially dangerous. One hears so many terrible reports, so many stories about bandits! Our Samaritan, who was a peddler by trade, was always on the road. But just like *Everyone*, he had common sense and managed not to be delayed.

So, our Samaritan was almost like Everyone. He did own a donkey, and not *Everyone* could boast about owning such a donkey.

Why the big fuss, you will say, about owning a donkey?

Well, first of all, this donkey was indispensable. It was used as a truck, since in those days trucks had four legs instead of four wheels as they do today. The donkey carried heavy merchandise for the Samaritan. It carried the Samaritan's whole wealth.

Second, this donkey was a female, a very important fact for the rest of the story.

Third, one reason the Samaritan was so original was that his donkey was not like *Everyone*. It had the Spirit of Contradiction.

Was the donkey, this female donkey, a descendant of Balaam's female donkey in the Old Testament? (Read Numbers 22 in the Bible.) Maybe. In any case, while other donkeys obeyed, this donkey was a thinking donkey, and its thoughts resulted in the most unexpected, the strangest, consequences.

Sometimes in the middle of the road, the donkey came to a dead stop, smelling something with its grey muzzle. It resisted so firmly that neither blows nor shouts could force it to walk any further.

Oftentimes the donkey did just the opposite. It took off at a trot, its nostrils open to the wind, and nothing could stop it, neither the calls nor the angry objections of its master. Had a special smell or a light on the horizon attracted it? Then the donkey would come back much later, having satisfied its taste for adventure.

Everyone felt sorry for the poor Samaritan for owning such a donkey. He who wanted desperately to look like everyone else, suffered severely to stand out so noticeably.

Ridiculous confrontations occurred so often between him and his donkey that in faraway villages, he was simply known as "the man with the donkey." People talked endlessly about his adventures.

But the most humiliating factor was that when the donkey opposed him and *Everyone* else, the stupid animal ended up being right.

How the Donkey Revolted Against the Rules of Social Conventions

Very late one evening, a man and a woman came to the door of the Samaritan. It was on the eve of the census ordered by the Governor Quirinius.

"Can't you take us in?" they asked. "We come from faraway and are very tired."

"Impossible," growled the Samaritan, thinking of his messy room. "Go elsewhere. There are hotels, and there are rich people with better lodging than I have."

"We just came from the village," answered the travelers, "and we knocked on every door. Everything is full. Wouldn't you have a place in your barn? We could sleep on the hay."

"I don't have a barn. I keep my hay in haystacks. I have only a stable."

"Oh! Put us in the stable," begged the woman. "I can't take one more step!"

"It is too little. Both of you would not fit in it," mumbled the peddler, lighting a torch to prove his point.

The stable was indeed very small and quite miserable. There was just enough room for the donkey that turned its head and stared at the flickering light of the torch with its big eyeballs.

"You see," said the owner, "it's impossible."

"If you only put a bale of straw under the manger, we could manage," suggested the woman.

ANGELS AND DONKEYS

Giving in to her persistence rather than to pity, the Samaritan accepted her idea. He untied the donkey to make it go out. For once, it would spend the night under the stars.

But the animal decided otherwise and launched a most ridiculous scene of stubbornness. Well planted on its four legs, eyes protruding, nostrils dilated, it refused to move.

The Samaritan was furious. One really shouldn't let people sleep under the muzzle of an animal. It is not correct! He kept jerking hard on the halter, swearing at the stupid animal. But knowing its habits, he knew ahead of time that he would not make the donkey budge.

"Nothing doing," he said after a while, shrugging his shoulders.

"Leave it there," said Mary with a smile. "We'll get along fine with it."

They got along so well, in fact, that the donkey became the quiet and patient witness of the birth of Jesus.

Joseph put the newborn child in the manger, above Mary. This way the breath of the dozing animal kept the child warm. Its big body also kept the stable warm so that the child and its mother didn't suffer anymore from the cold.

When he opened the door the next morning, the bewildered Samaritan discovered that the two travelers of the previous evening had become three.

"It is lucky my donkey refused to get out," said he to Joseph. "The frost was so deep last night that without her in the stable, the newborn child would certainly have died from the cold!"

"Once more," he murmured on his way home, "it is the donkey who was right and not me."

How the Donkey Taught Its Master About Helping Strangers

Ten days later, Mary was up and nearly back to her normal health. Joseph was thinking about returning to Nazareth when, during the night, he was divinely warned of the threat hanging over the child's head. They must flee, he was told, before morning comes; they must go to Egypt.

He woke Mary, but soon realized that she wasn't yet strong enough to take such a long trip on foot.

Joseph knocked on the door of the Samaritan.

"Lend me your donkey for one month," said he, "or for six weeks at the most. We must flee to Egypt and my wife is still weary."

"Don't even dream of it," answered the Samaritan. "I need my donkey to make a living, and also . . . I don't know you. How do I know you would bring it back?"

"I promise," said Joseph. "You can count on me."

"No way," cut in the Samaritan. "Can I trust the word of a stranger? The answer is no!"

Very worried, the new parents and their baby started out before dawn. Joseph walked ahead making the trail. Mary followed, stumbling sometimes as she carried the child.

But what was the galloping sound they heard from far away? Were Herod's soldiers pursuing them? Already?

No, it was the donkey who soon caught up with them, sniffing them in the night with its wet muzzle. Possessed by one of its wild whims, the donkey had gnawed at its tie, escaped from the stable, and left on its night adventure.

Awakened by the noise, the Samaritan went out, calling his animal back, but without success. "It followed those strangers," he exclaimed furiously. "Well, I have to resign myself to the loss. Ah, cursed be that animal! What will become of me without it to work?"

Six weeks later, Herod had died and the Samaritan looked up to see Joseph walking toward him. Mary sat on the donkey, holding the child.

"Your animal saved us," said Joseph.

"Without it, my wife could not have gone very far. The king's soldiers would have discovered us and killed the child."

"I was wrong again," said the peddler to himself, full of gratefulness. "There are some honest people, even among strangers! One must learn to trust them. It is God's way."

How the Donkey Taught Its Master Courage

Several years went by. Conflicts between the donkey and its master became less frequent. Not that the animal had become more reasonable; instead its master had, little by little, fallen into the habit of obeying the donkey. Its lunacy seemed wiser than the man's good sense.

One evening, and contrary to his habit, the Samaritan was delayed between Jerusalem and Jericho. His trip almost turned into tragedy.

He had heard about a band of robbers operating in that area, demanding money from travelers, that is, if they didn't kill them outright.

It was nightfall. The Samaritan spurred his animal on, exciting it as much as possible. Often he thought he heard soft steps behind him.

Suddenly, the animal started one of its caprices and refused to advance any further. First the peddler pulled on the bridle. Then overtaken by fear, he turned nasty. He tore the flesh in the donkey's mouth by jerking the bit roughly. Nothing changed the donkey's mind.

Discouraged, he stopped and started thinking. He thought of fleeing, of abandoning the animal and its precious cargo when, in the silence, he heard a moan. He was not superstitious, but the noise in the darkness filled him with terror. Once more he tried to drag the animal along, but with its muzzle on the ground, it arched its back and obstinately dug its hooves into the ground.

The moaning became a long wail. The Samaritan thought he detected a call coming from a ravine below the road. He thought to himself, "What if the donkey was right once more?" Mastering his fear, he walked down among the boulders and found an injured man who would die if he got no help. Using oil and wine, he dressed the wounds of this unfortunate man, hoisted him up on his donkey, and immediately took him to the nearest inn. He watched over him through the night. Whenever he saw him weaken, he poured a cordial between his clenched teeth to give him strength.

The next morning the wounded man felt better. Convinced that the donkey had shown him what God wanted, the Samaritan pulled out nearly all the cash he had, gave it to the innkeeper and said, "Take care of him. If you spend more than that, I'll pay you on my way back."

Although the innkeeper had no donkey to advise him, he trusted the Samaritan.

How the Donkey Found What It Was Looking For

Thirty years went by. The Samaritan had left Bethlehem and moved to Bethphage by the gates of Jerusalem. It was a better location for his business.

The donkey was still alive. Donkeys live long, sometimes for 35 years. But this one's legs had become shaky and its flanks had lost their luster and their fullness. Yet it was still the same courageous animal, only a little less original. In its mysterious animal consciousness, it had always looked for something, expected something. That's why it had not been like *Everyone*, docile like those who do not look for anything.

Now death was approaching, and the donkey had not found what it was looking for, neither in the tufts of grass nor on the distant horizon.

The donkey found some compensation, however. It had given birth to a little donkey, a shaggy and petulant foal of which she was most proud. It was already strong and would soon be ready to work. The mother donkey had begun dreaming something like this: "He'll be the one to find what I always looked for."

Old people console themselves with comforting thoughts, hoping their children will some day accomplish what they haven't done themselves. And those children, when they grow old, will nurture the same dream. So it is with each generation.

So one day, the donkey and its foal were tethered in front of their master's dwelling in Bethphage. Two men appeared, put their hands on the bridles, and appeared to be about to take the animals away.

The Samaritan made a big racket. Flying out of his room, he yelled to the passersby, "Thief! Thief!"

"The Lord needs them," the two strangers kept repeating.

"The Lord? The Lord? And who is the

Lord?" shouted the indignant peddler. "These animals are mine. And, who are you? I don't know you."

"We'll return them to you," said the two men, who did look honest. "You can count on us."

The Samaritan was about ready to end the discussion with his usual answer—"No, the answer is no!"—when a faint memory came back to him of a man and woman, and his refusal to lend them his donkey long ago. They were strangers, and *Everyone* would have done the same. You can't trust anybody. But then the donkey had run away, and it had been right in the end.

"Pull the old donkey by the bridle," he told the men. "It doesn't know you. If it obeys you, well . . . then we'll see!"

The man who held the donkey pulled, and the docile animal followed him, while its little foal trotted alongside.

When they were a short distance away, the peddler shouted to the disciples, "Take it to

ANGELS AND DONKEYS

your Lord! This animal is always right!"

And without worrying anymore, he went into his house.

As the prophet predicted, it was at the Bethphage gate that Jesus saw the donkey and its foal coming toward him. (The story is in Matthew 21:1-9.) Along the roadside, he picked a bunch of fragrant grass and offered it to the old donkey.

The donkey smelled it longingly with its grey muzzle. This was exactly what it had always looked for. A hundred times through the years it had trotted on this very same path and had hastily grazed this kind of grass. But today the grass held a new fragrance and flavor.

In their confused minds, as you know, animals see God less clearly than we do. They see God through their masters. This time, from the hand of the true Master, the donkey received the nourishment it had always hoped to find.

Jesus straddled the young donkey "which had never before been ridden." The crowd spread clothing under its steps, and the old donkey followed behind, trampling it with its hooves.

A multitude of disciples waved palm branches, crying out, "Blessed be the kingdom which is coming, the kingdom of David, our father!"

When the procession reached the slope of the Mount of Olives, the old donkey noticed the white wall of Jerusalem. Through the years the donkey had traveled this path countless times, setting its eyes on the spectacle with the indifference common to animals. But today, these brilliant walls shining on the horizon seemed to be the sides of a *Stable* which it had always dreamed about and looked for.

The donkey raised its head and walked ahead more bravely.

Yet there was even more for the animal than the satisfaction carried by the fragrant grass and the vision of the *Stable*. On that morning, the old donkey also experienced the noblest of joys. It found itself in the middle of a large crowd acclaiming a King. And it had become the servant of this Prince who, it believed, was truly noble and truly good.

The old donkey's soul felt overwhelmed with joy. True, the Creator had assigned the animal to the humblest of duties, but it saw its little donkey assigned to a place of honor. Until death came, the old donkey would happily remain in last place, following the steps of its own offspring.

So why do you think donkeys have the Spirit of Contradiction? Because the young donkey inherited his mother's temperament. Later on, he married and had lots of children.

The Church Built with Snow

a story about living honorably,
told to a small mountain village
contending with Hitler's threat

The First Day

It snowed a lot that year—40 centimeters of heavy snow, wet, and well packed. The children were overjoyed.

On Christmas Eve, the schoolmaster gathered his students together before he went away for the holidays.

"My children," said he, "I am leaving for 10 days. You are going to be free of school. Try to put your vacation to good use. I am not giving you any homework, but I am counting on all of you—Little Ones, Middle Ones, and Big Ones—to prepare a beautiful surprise for me. I'll find it when I return. All right?"

"Yes, sir!" exclaimed the schoolchildren in one voice.

The Second Day—
The Church Built with Snow

The following day was Christmas. The sun shone on the snow. The Little Ones met on the square for a consultation in front of the school. "I," said the smallest of the Little Ones, "I have an idea. Why don't we build a church for the Master made entirely of snow?"

"Yes, yes!" approved the other Little Ones, clapping their hands. And they scattered to fetch shovels and pickaxes, spades and sleds

ANGELS AND DONKEYS

to shape and transport the bricks made of snow. They were going to build a magnificent church of snow.

Towards evening, the church was finished, and the Middle Ones and the Big Ones came to admire it.

It was a very beautiful church of snow, for the Little Ones had put all their love into it. It was so tall that the Little Ones could enter it without bending down, and the Middle Ones and the Big Ones could stand up almost straight in it. They had to bend their heads only a bit. But a church is made for prayer anyway, and everyone agreed everything was very well done.

The church even had windows, with panes made of thin ice the Little Ones had harvested from the pond.

When night closed in, the Little Ones lit a Christmas tree in their church. They worshiped and sang songs. The tree could be seen from the outside through the panes made of ice, and the music could be heard through the door. All the grown-ups came out of their houses to listen. Tears of contentment filled their eyes, so moved were they by what the Little Ones had done. All thought of joy, the joy of the Master upon his return when he would see the surprise.

But the Middle Ones became jealous of their little friends and decided to do better.

The Third Day— The Palace Built with Snow

On the third day, the Middle Ones met on the school square and had a consultation.

"I," said the most average of the Middle Ones who had gone to the movies in the city, "I have an idea. How about building a palace made entirely of snow for the Master? A Snow White's palace!"

"Yes, yes!" exclaimed the Middle Ones clapping their hands, and they went to fetch shovels and pickaxes, spades and sleds to shape and transport bricks made of snow. They were about to build a magnificent palace of snow.

Towards evening, the palace was finished, and the Small Ones and the Big Ones came to admire it.

It was a beautiful palace because the Middle Ones had put all their intelligence into it. The palace had several rooms, each one taller and larger than the Little Ones' church. There were doors to go from one room to the others. There were windows made of ice panes like in the church. There were snow bridges strong enough to walk across. The palace even had towers, but it was better not to climb on them since that made them fall down. Each tower was topped with a big, pointy icicle lightning rod.

When night closed in, the Middle Ones organized a celebration in their palace, an overnight party with Chinese lanterns and songs. The most average of the Middle Ones told the story of Snow White, another recited poems, yet another gave a speech to prove that the idea of the Middle Ones was better than the idea of the Little Ones, and that Snow White's palace was better built than the church because there were several larger rooms, all different. All the Middle Ones applauded, congratulating each other for having been so intelligent.

The Little Ones were saddened because no one was looking at the church anymore. But the Big Ones became jealous of the Middle Ones and decided to do better yet.

The Fourth Day— The Fort Built with Snow

On the fourth day, the Big Ones met on the school square and had a consultation.

"I," said the biggest one of the Big Ones, "I think the Little Ones and the Middle Ones play like girls with their church and their fairy-tale palace. As for us, we are men, and we are going to play like men! How about building a fort made of snow?"

"Yes, yes," exclaimed the Big Ones without clapping their hands, for fear of looking ridiculous. And they went to fetch shovels and pickaxes, spades and sleds to shape and transport large bricks of snow, much bigger than the ones used by the Little Ones and the Middle Ones. They were preparing to construct a magnificent snow fort.

Toward evening, the fort was finished, and the Little Ones and the Middle Ones came to visit it. But in front of the door was posted a sentinel with a big stick, who said, "No entry! Get away from here you little mosquitoes. The fort is only for the Big Ones."

A bit frightened, the Little Ones and the Middle Ones backed off, satisfied to look at the fort from afar. The snow fort was very handsome because the Big Ones had used all their strength. It had enormous walls, twice as tall as any one of them, with notched battlements framing the threatening faces of the Big Ones keeping watch.

When night closed in, the Big Ones started to walk in the courtyard of the fort, stepping in rhythm to the sound of wild music with loud cymbal crashes. (They used covers of pots and pans picked up in the trash.) Those outside the fort could hear rough words of commands from within, followed by periods of silence. Then the noise would start again. It was grandiose.

The Fifth Day

On the fifth day, the Little Ones, the Middle Ones, and the Big Ones started to get bored. The most patient ones fussed over and decorated their masterpieces, but most of them went back to their usual games. They forgot their promise to the Master.

Then the biggest one of the Big Ones shouted, "I have lots of extra energy and nothing to do. Let's play war!"

A yell of excitement answered him. The Big Ones started immediately to gather a stock of snowballs in their fort. They built small walls facing Snow White's palace so they could throw snowballs, yet be protected.

When they were all prepared, the Middle Ones shrugged their shoulders, trying to convince themselves that they were intelligent and had nothing to fear from the strength of the Big Ones. But a few of them were scared and quickly tried to build up their stock of snowballs behind the walls of their palace. And so, the fifth day ended.

The Sixth Day

The War started in the middle of the sixth day. At the signal, the Big Ones came out of their fort and bombarded the Middle Ones with snowballs. Smiling at first, the Middle Ones returned the blows. But the Big Ones were strong. Their snowballs pummeled the palace of snow, broke through the ice panes and knocked down pinnacles and turrets. The Middle Ones' snowballs proved powerless against the fort's ramparts. The Middle Ones became furious at the harm the Big Ones inflicted on their building. And so they put stones inside their snowballs. There was blood on the faces of the Big Ones. The biggest of the Big Ones accused the Middle Ones of planning harm, and he ordered an attack.

The Big Ones took possession of Snow White's palace, they ransacked it, trampled it down, and leveled it. They kicked and punched the Middle Ones who tried their best to stop them.

And what were the Little Ones doing? First they tried not to see what was happening. They locked themselves up in their church and sang hymns. But when the first lost snowball shattered one of their ice windows, they understood this affair was also their business. So they picked up their Christmas tree and formed a procession, trying to stand between the Big Ones and the Middle Ones. And they shouted, "Stop! Interrupt the fight! Don't ruin the beautiful surprises we all prepared for our Master's return! You are going to make our beloved teacher very sad!"

But their voices were too weak and no one listened to them. Instead, the Middle Ones joined the Big Ones to attack the Little Ones. And the handsome church of snow was ransacked, destroyed, and leveled.

Towards evening, no one was left on the battlefield. The Little Ones and the Middle Ones had black eyes, split lips, and broken teeth. They all fled home. The Big Ones retreated to their fort, proudly exhibiting their glorious wounds.

Suddenly, their sentinel shouted in the night. He raised his arm and pointed towards the school. A light had just appeared in their Master's window. The Big Ones, the Middle Ones, and the Little Ones started to shake. "The Master returned when we didn't expect him! The Master will see everything tomorrow morning. He will punish us! We don't have time to rebuild!"

But the biggest of the Big Ones smiled and asked his fellow Big Ones, "Dummies that you are, why are you trembling? It is the Middle Ones and the Small Ones who will be scolded. Our fort will stand for eternity. The Master will have to bow in front of our might, just like anyone else!" And in the black night sky a black cloth flapped at the top of a lean pole. It was the Big One's banner.

The Seventh Day

In the middle of the night, while everyone slept, a Southern wind started to blow; its long wailings reverberated down chimneys. A warm rain from the South fell, melting all the snow. It washed away the ruins of the church and the ruins of the palace. It even washed away the fortress full of pride. Nothing was left.

ANGELS AND DONKEYS

When morning came, the Master assembled his students.

"Poor children," said he, "you built with snow! Don't you know that snow melts in the Southern wind? Your masterpieces weren't worth much. They were just games for which I have no use. But your intentions are what matter to me. Show me your eyes so that I may read what lies in the depth of your hearts."

The Big Ones came first, and the Master said, "I read in your eyes power and pride. You built an enormous fort, and you destroyed your friends' masterpieces. Go and see what's left of your fortress." And the Big Ones found nothing. Nothing but nothingness.

The Middle Ones came next. The Master said, "I read in your eyes intelligence, but the kind of intelligence that is made of extravagance and vanity. You had an idea, and you believed in the power of that idea. But when the Big Ones attacked you, you gave up your idea. It was just wind. Go see what's left of your palace." And the Middle Ones found only a swamp of melting snow where their palace used to stand.

Then came the Little Ones. "Your eyes," said the master, "are full of sadness and shame. You built a church, but it was a church made only of snow. Nothing of it is left today. You tried to stop the battle, and you didn't succeed. Go and see the place where your church stood!" The Little Ones went out to the site of their church. And next to the puddle that had been their church, they found a little bit of grass, already turning green. It was the first announcement of Spring.

The Revolt of the Animals

*a story about resisting nonviolently,
about the madness
of some humans,
and about the importance
of each individual's contribution*

This is not a Christmas story.

The revolt started a few days ago in a barn somewhere in the nearby mountains.

I ask you, why are peasants so foolhardy as to leave the door open that separates their kitchen from the animal barn? (In Haute-

Loire, people and farm animals lived at
opposite ends of one long farm building.)
Now that there is a radio in every farm, the
animals overhear things they should not
know. Of course, not all understand the
language of human beings. But in the farm
we are talking about, there was a very wise
old cow. Because she was repeatedly insulted
by her drunken master, she had learned
French! What she heard over the radio made
her indignant.

Listen to her discussion with her neighbor,
an old horse, about her age: "I can't
understand anymore what the good Lord,
father of all people and animals, is doing. My
mother taught me that human beings are
wiser than we are, and, at the time of
creation, God allowed them to rule over us.
He ordered us to be obedient and docile. We
give the milk of our children to feed their
children, we pull their wagons and plows,
and we sacrifice our lives so they may eat our
flesh and shape shoes from our pelts. I just

overheard that my master will soon take me to the House From Which No One Returns because I am too old to give him milk!"

"As for me," answered the horse, "my eyes are starting to cloud over, and I know they are digging a trench in which they'll bury me."

"Of course," started the cow again, "as long as humans seemed wise, I was willing to be obedient. But today, after listening to their speaking machine, I realize they are crazier than we are. I thought they killed only to eat like tigers do, because it is their law. But now I realize they kill each other for pleasure, and that they let bodies lie on the ground to rot. All this is absurd. I don't want to work for them anymore. I don't want to die for people anymore."

"But you can't revolt alone, against the opinion of all the others," answered the horse. "Look at the other animals, how docile they are. The dog runs when his master calls him and orders him to bite the legs of the cattle. As for us horses, they jam a bit in our mouths.

And on you cows, they place a yoke on your heads. (In central France the wooden yoke was strapped to the horns of the animals who pulled plows with their heads, not with their necks.) We pull, we walk, we stop, we stand still in place, sometimes for hours, according to our master's fancy, when we could simply kill him with a strong kick. But what's the use of doing things differently than God's law?"

"Well then, we must ask God to change the law," said the cow. "He needs to be spoken to. Let me do it."

The next day as she grazed in the fields, the cow called the skylark out of her furrow. They had a long conversation; then the skylark darted through the air, straight up in the sky. As she flew farther up, her trills became weaker to the ear until they completely vanished.

The skylark landed on God's knee. With a smile, the creator picked her up and brought her to his ear. The skylark shared with him the grievances of the animals.

"So be it," answered God, and, thinking about humanity, his expression grew gloomy. "You have my permission to revolt. But I forbid you to hurt the lives of human beings. We have enough blood spilled on the earth as it is."

The skylark dropped back down to earth next to the cow. Upon hearing the news, the cow said, "Summon to this spot tomorrow morning all the birds of the world. Let the news be transmitted from beak to bill."

"What were you plotting with the skylark?" asked the horse after nightfall.

"You'll see tomorrow morning," answered the cow.

The next day, very early, the sky was black with birds. When the peasant and his wife came out of their house they were terrorized. Everywhere were birds of all sizes and all colors, from royal eagles to hummingbirds, from nightingales with their rusty plumage to flashing birds of paradise.

"Go quickly around the world," the cow told them. "Announce to all animals that God is allowing them to revolt against humanity. Hostilities will be unleashed in exactly a week, at six o'clock in the morning. However, no one is permitted to kill a person. That is forbidden by God!"

So the birds dispersed, and for seven days the earth returned to normal.

But after a week . . .

All the peasants in the world were stunned when their horses and cows refused to be harnessed and yoked. These animals, which they always assumed were stupid, proudly raised their heads, shaking off their halters. They shot their disorderly tails up in the air and took off for the bushes. (The French uses the word *maquis*, also the name of the underground movement during World War II.) The peasants tried to send their dogs after them, but the dogs left with strange smiles on their pendulous lips, and they didn't come back.

The peasants said to themselves, "Don't worry! We'll see them come back when mealtime comes around!" But they were wrong. The animals didn't return.

So the farmers said, "Let's organize a hunt. We'll bring along ropes and chains to force the rebels back."

Looking quite relaxed, the animals let the men come close to them, but as soon as they thought they held them fast, the animals bucked and took off on a trot. Others galloped through the line the peasants had formed, knocked them over in the mud, and then ran away out of sight.

Frightened by now, the men decided that at any price, they would recover their authority over the animals, and so they declared war. They gathered millions of soldiers under the command of their most famous generals. For the first time, the whole of humanity united against a common danger. They put their tanks out in the fields and took out their cannons and their airplanes. "We'll kill a few," they reasoned, "then the others will submit."

But it didn't happen. The animals were first in launching the offensive. At night while the human beings were asleep, the rabbits invaded their fields and devoured everything they found: green wheat, beets, cabbage, carrots, vegetables of all kinds. It was a hunger blockade in a new style. In the morning when the peasants woke up, their gardens were a desert, and the enemy had vanished.

Then the men decided to exterminate all the animals. They conceived a battle campaign. But the gnats and the ants which can sneak everywhere became spies. Each time an army thought it was about to surround a large gathering of animals, it found the place empty. The enemy had fled.

It was the most amusing, the most unexpected, of all wars. Each animal had its role to play; each had its responsibilities.

What did the little birds do? They became

express messengers. They delivered all the commands of the old cow.

And the big birds? They became observation planes, discovering the movements of the adversary.

The owls? They became night fighters.

The dogs? Sentinels, faithfully keeping watch, and company sergeants in charge of discipline.

The cats? Scouts advancing without noise toward the enemy.

The roosters? Clarions.

The goats? Mountain troops.

The horses? Cavalry.

The cows? Infantrymen.

The rhinoceroses? Tanks.

The crocodiles? Submarines.

The giraffes? Observers.

The bees? Providers of food and services.

The parrots? Speakers on the radio spreading "the word."

The chameleons? Specialists in camouflage.

The lions and tigers? Spreaders of terror

among the adversaries' ranks.

The moles? Miners whose persistent digging brought the enemy's trenches and houses down.

And the mosquitoes? Guerrillas who pestered the rear guard.

The war didn't last long. Deprived of meat, milk, butter, and all the products grown in fields, the human beings dragged themselves through their idle cities and their devastated villages. Their armaments proved powerless against the animals. It was their turn to implore God.

And God answered them. "The animals are right. They are willing to obey you, but upon one condition—that you become wiser than they are. Give up killing each other, and the animals will again submit to you."

"So be it!" answered the human beings.

The armistice was decided, and a peace treaty was soon signed. The old order returned. The animals became docile again and resumed their services to people. The old cow died courageously, giving her flesh as food. The humans didn't thank her. But they discharged their armies, covered their generals with decorations, and retired them.

As for the army barracks, they were locked up and replaced by schools and churches.

The Slave Set Free

*a story about whether good
is stronger than evil*

The Slave

At the bottom of the enormous wall of the
Temple in Jerusalem, dust from the
market square sparkled in the young April sun.

It was the day following the great Jewish
Feast of the Passover celebration. The normal
activity of daily life had started again in the city.
At one end of the square, shouting children
played hopscotch, while, at the other end,
slaves were being sold on a wooden platform.

Sales were going well and the merchant was happy. He was soon left with only one more head to sell—a man of about 25, whose white hands and puny body indicated that he was not trained to work in the fields. One could detect shame on his face, for he was not accustomed to having shackled wrists and ankles.

"Come on, let's hurry," barked the merchant. "Help me get rid of Thaddeus, an educated slave who is exceptionally intelligent and capable!"

"Too intelligent," joked a rich tradesman walking by. "You know that as late as yesterday, Thaddeus was the administrator of Herod Antipas' palace. He stole enormous sums of money. I'd worry that he would ruin me if I trusted him with the smallest of my businesses."

"Buy Thaddeus for any amount! I'm closing shop. Who is ready to make an offer?" shouted the merchant.

"If I let him in my household, he would cause all sorts of conflicts," commented a

Pharisee in a white robe. "Thaddeus was an informer. He reported his co-workers' peccadilloes to the king—just so he would look good. Antipas put up with his swindling money because Thaddeus became a very useful servant. Once he even tried to strangle one of the king's buddies who owed Herod Antipas 100 denarii! When the king was informed of the incident he sold Thaddeus into slavery! That's the man's story."

"I'll give you Thaddeus for half price," moaned the merchant. "Come on, who'll take him off my hands for 50 denarii? Fifty denarii? Fifteen silver coins? That's nothing nowadays!"

A stranger came forward. His face had been slashed many times.

"For that price, give him to me," he roared. "I'll send him to die in the copper mines I own on Cyprus. The way he looks, he won't last longer than three months!"

But a piercing scream suddenly rose from the last row of the crowd. "No!"

Everyone turned to see who had shrieked. It was a young boy about 12 years old with blue eyes and bushy hair. He wore a coarse, woolen tunic like farmers did in Galilee. A few minutes before, he had been playing hopscotch at the other end of the square.

"No," the child repeated in a chilling voice, like someone calling for help. "I don't want him to go to the mines. I'll buy him for 60 denarii."

The crowd burst out laughing.

"I never sold a slave to a child yet," sneered the merchant. "Do you have the money?"

Splitting the crowd apart, the child came forward. Little silver coins glittered in the coil of his belt.

"Seventy denarii!" growled the scar-faced man loudly.

"Eighty," shouted the child, jumping up on the platform.

"Ninety!" howled the other.

"One hundred!" exclaimed the child, his voice breaking with emotion because that was all he had. In one gesture, he loosened his belt and emptied it, spreading its contents on the merchant's table—30 pieces of good silver, witnessed by everyone.

"Who bids higher? Who bids higher?" repeated the merchant, hoping to raise the bids even more.

But no one spoke. The man with the brutal face shrugged his shoulders, mumbling as he walked away, "The wretch isn't worth it!"

"Well," said the merchant, shaking the child who stood motionless, as if numbed by his victory, "take your slave. He's yours. Here is your certificate of ownership, written on a sheet of Egyptian papyrus. Just lead him away by his chain."

Then the crowd saw a most amazing thing happen. Thaddeus, one of the shrewdest and most feared men in Jerusalem, offered his shackled wrists to a young boy who deliberately but gently pulled him along, as one would a young sheep just purchased on the marketplace.

The Redeemed

When they were alone, Thaddeus asked his new master, "Why did you buy me?"

"I bought you because I am going to become a great chief who will lead hundreds—thousands—of men. When I saw you so sad, I thought you could become the first of my servants."

"But you aren't rich," objected Thaddeus. "For a little peasant, you paid an enormous sum to own me."

"I spent everything I owned," answered the child calmly. "The money was a treasure I received when I was born. Now that I am 12, my parents had me accompany them to Jerusalem. They gave me my money so I could enter a school to become a scribe and study the Holy Scriptures."

"I'm not worth what you paid for me," said Thaddeus wearily, "and now you're destitute. How will you pay for your education?"

"When I saw you," said the child, "I knew you were worth more than my studies. I'm not worried about having no more money now that I own a servant like you. Do you believe in God?"

"I used to believe when I was your age," mumbled Thaddeus. "But then something horrible happened, and I can't believe anymore."

"Tell me what happened," said the child with interest.

"Well, it was about 12 years ago. I kept my sheep in a field near Bethlehem, Judea, with my father and uncles. One night an angel appeared and told us, 'Do not be afraid. I bring you good news which will bring a great joy to all people. Today the Messiah of Israel was born in a stable in the city of David.' So we ran to Bethlehem where we found exactly what the angel had told us, and we worshiped the Savior of the World."

"But that's no reason to lose your faith!" interrupted the child. "On the contrary, you should be living with great joy!"

"Unfortunately," answered Thaddeus, "my story isn't finished. A few weeks later as we tended our sheep in the same fields, we heard shouts and wailings during the night. It was the women of Bethlehem calling for help. We ran towards the city but we got there too late. King Herod the Great had ordered that all the baby boys should be killed because he was insanely jealous. He got wildly envious when he learned the future King of Israel was one of these children. Panic-stricken, moaning mothers were trying to find their own babies. The stable where we had worshiped the Messiah was burning in the night. The manger where the child had slept was knocked over. In the distance we could still hear the king's soldiers galloping toward Jerusalem."

"I am beginning to understand what you are saying," murmured the young boy.

"If God allows such things," continued Thaddeus somberly, "if he lets the Messiah be killed without stopping the killer, that means God is too weak to have his will done on earth. It is since that day that I don't believe in God's existence anymore."

"So what did you do?" asked the child.

"I fled from Bethlehem and entered the service of King Herod the Great, who showed himself to be stronger than God. He was Herod the Cruel, Herod the Rich, and he was never stopped by any scruples when defending his throne. At his school I learned how to cheat and how to lie—the way the weak make their way in the world.

"After his death I remained in the palace, serving his son Herod Antipas. By spying on my friends and betraying them, I obtained favors from the King. Step by step, I rose to the highest position. I became administrator of the Palace in Jerusalem. You know the rest about my downfall from the mouths of the people insulting me a while ago. Boy, now you know everything."

The Freedman

After these confessions, the man and the
boy walked a long time without speaking.
They had passed the workshop of Tubalcain
the blacksmith and had reached the road to
Tyropeon, when the boy suddenly changed
his mind. He stopped, insisted that
Thaddeus retrace his steps, and made him
enter the blacksmith's shop.

"I don't have any money to pay you," he
said to Tubalcain with great firmness, "but
my slave and I, we are asking you for a
favor. Cut the chains that bind his hands and
feet."

"That's not customary, young master,"
objected Tubalcain. "Your slave could easily
run away."

"That's too bad then. Let him run away! I
don't want to own a slave anymore. I want
to free this man."

"You're setting me free!" exclaimed
Thaddeus, amazed. "But you just spent a

fortune to buy me! Didn't you say I would be the first one of many servants you would command some day?"

"Yes, but I want all those people to join me on their own," answered the young boy, "without being forced. If you continue to be my slave, you would *have* to obey me. So cut those chains!" he ordered the blacksmith in a tone that didn't allow any discussion.

Tubalcain obeyed.

When he was done, Thaddeus didn't move. He did not know what to do with his freedom. "Where should I go?" he asked himself. "I just found a master, my first friend on earth, and I am already losing him!" Perplexed, he looked at his wrists and ankles where the chains had left the red marks of shame.

The boy was already gone. Through the door, Thaddeus could see him running, laughing, clapping his hands, and shouting:

"Good-bye, Thaddeus. I'm so happy you are free. Maybe we'll meet again some day!"

The Slave Set Free   **111**

The Adopted

The youngster was about to disappear, and Thaddeus suddenly realized he might never see him again. He started to run after him. The young boy stopped.

"Don't leave me alone, I beg you," shouted Thaddeus. "I want to stay with you. I will serve you freely."

The boy did not answer but stretched out his hand to the slave. Thaddeus placed his full-grown hand in the little hand of the boy with the confidence of a son in his father.

"I'll follow you wherever you go," said Thaddeus.

"In that case," said the boy, who never seemed astonished, "I won't call you my servant anymore, but my friend. Come, let's tell all this to my father."

And he took Thaddeus with him toward the highest part of the city where the rich people lived and where God's temple was located. "Could he be the son of a prince disguised as a peasant?" wondered Thaddeus. "Is he going to introduce me to his father as his friend and not his slave? One can expect anything from this extraordinary boy. . ."

Arriving at the next intersection, the boy turned right toward God's temple. They walked diagonally across the open space in front of the temple, the part that is surrounded with porticoes. They climbed the steps which lead through the Beautiful Portal gateway to the women's enclosure, and then to the enclosure of the men of Israel.

From there they climbed another 15 steps and went through the gateway that took them to the courtyard of the priests. They walked around the altar used for sacrifices and stopped at the entrance to the Holy Place.

In the back of the dark sanctuary, a sumptuous curtain protects the very Holy Place where the High Priest himself enters only once a year, on the Day of Expiations.

"We have arrived in my father's house," whispered the boy, and Thaddeus noticed a strange light shining in his face. Beyond the curtain, the young boy seemed to gaze on someone whom Thaddeus could not see. He conversed with this invisible being, and occasionally his lips moved.

Then in a very soft yet firm voice, the boy started to speak so distinctly that Thaddeus understood every word: "Father," he said, "I brought you Thaddeus, my friend. He sinned a lot, but he also suffered a lot. When he was my age, he lost his faith. He was scandalized because he thought I had died under the swords of Herod's soldiers. But here I am, Father, alive in front of you because you rescued me.

"In the same way, Father, I just rescued Thaddeus from Satan's hands, Satan who had made him a slave. I redeemed him and freed him of all obligations towards me, towards any other man, and even towards you, my father.

"However, Father, this free man has voluntarily chosen to follow me. So I am asking you—I, your only son—to adopt

ANGELS AND DONKEYS

Thaddeus as your child, as if he were your own son. Wherever I might be, I want him to be my brother forever. I may ask you this favor, Father, since I paid the ransom money for his freedom."

In the great silence that followed that prayer, no voice from heaven was heard, but a marvelous dawn was born in Thaddeus' heart. All doubts, bitterness, and traces of blood left by the horror in Bethlehem started to disappear like nightmares at sunrise.

Thaddeus could now absorb the sun in its whole glory. It was God himself whose shining love, fatherly tenderness, and redeeming forgiveness washed over him like waves of an ocean made of light. His heart filled with gratefulness, like a bud swollen with sap in the spring. Words sprung from within him rose to his lips, words of prayer he could never have pronounced before: "My father," said his heart, "my father, I am your son, and yet I am not worthy enough to be called your son. . ."

The Son

Shouting noises interrupted Thaddeus' meditation. He shivered and then realized the young boy had left his side.

He turned around and saw him at the bottom of the steps in the women's courtyard, in the middle of a group of agitated scribes and doctors of law speaking all at once.

He feared his friend was in danger and rushed to his help. But he stopped suddenly, as soon as he understood the reason for all this disturbance. In the middle of the crowd, a Galilean peasant, no doubt the boy's father, kept shaking his son vigorously.

"Jesus, my child, how could you do this to us? You disappeared without a word, and you even lost the Wise Men's treasure we had given you. You are 12, and I thought you deserved our total trust. You have never disappointed us. Say good-bye to your schooling now. We are taking you back to

ANGELS AND DONKEYS

Nazareth. You'll be a carpenter, just like me."

Jesus' mother kept kissing him, stroking his unkempt hair while crying and saying, "My little one, we found you. For three days your father and I have looked for you with great anguish."

Seeing him standing there between his father and his mother, Thaddeus realized the young boy was a child who that very morning was playing hopscotch and shouting happily with his friends.

Yet even in the hubbub of this reunion, the young boy's voice rose suddenly, so clear, so calm, that everyone kept respectfully quiet. "Why were you looking for me?" he asked his parents. "Don't you know I am supposed to attend to my father's business?" The doctors of law shook their heads. Joseph raised his eyes towards the sky. Mary lowered hers towards the ground, but it was quite evident that none of them understood what Jesus meant.

Thaddeus was the only one who did, repeating to himself, "The concerns Jesus has are God's affairs, and Jesus will minister to all of them. He will free all slaves by paying their ransoms." Meanwhile, the docile young boy left the courtyard between his father and his mother.

Just as he was ready to disappear out of sight, Jesus turned around and smiled. "You understand me, Thaddeus, my brother, my friend," his smile said. "Some day, I will come back for you."

The Wait

Thaddeus, the redeemed, free man, the brother of the Lord, the adopted son of God, waited patiently for the time his Messiah would come back for him.

He gave up his life of cheating and all his wealth, and he went to Galilee to help his brothers. In Capernaum near the synagogue, he opened a public writing boutique. For very little money, he wrote letters for people who did not know how to write. And in his mind he followed his little Messiah, who from year to year was growing in wisdom, size, and grace.

The years went by, and Thaddeus was now over 40 years old. He was like all the other just, pious men of his generation, waiting for the consolation of Israel, questioning with his eyes all the young men who walked by his shop, and wondering, "Is that the Messiah?"

One ordinary day just like all others, Thaddeus sat at his desk writing. And behold, a hand suddenly rested on his shoulder. Thaddeus didn't even need to look up. He recognized the voice that was calling him, "Follow me!" Thaddeus did not even turn his head.

He carefully put away the papyruses and stilettos covering his table. He stood up, shook his robe loose, wrapped a leather belt around his hips, went out on the street, closed the door behind him, and, without ever looking back, he willingly followed Jesus, his master.

The Slave Set Free

The Little Angel Who Didn't Sing

*a story about being jealous
and the damage that can cause*

In those times, among the multitude of Heavenly Beings, there was a Little Angel. His beauty was immaterial, like the beauty of all celestial creatures, and his soul was as limpid as a dewdrop. The other angels, servants of the Most High Lord, saved their sweetest smiles and their most foolish indulgences for him.

The younger angels were messengers and couriers. They constantly streaked from one

121

star to another through the ether to deliver the daily instructions. They called the Little Angel from far away to play with them. The adult angels were in charge of a province in the celestial spaces, the home of the sun, nebula, and constellations. They brought the Little Angel presents of flowers they picked on distant shores. As for the archangels who remained constantly in the presence of the Lord and who moved only on very rare occasions, they called the Little Angel to them and bounced him on their laps.

But it is not good to be spoiled, not even for a Little Angel to be spoiled. We know, of course, that the devil has no access to the Kingdom of Heaven where God's children are protected against all his blows. However, because he had been so pampered, the Little Angel had become capricious. And since in Up Above it is not customary to control a person, the Heavenly Beings simply smiled softly.

On the night Jesus was born, a great clamor resounded in Heaven, and the angels

ANGELS AND DONKEYS

of God assembled from the most distant regions to go down to earth and bring the Christmas message to all people. They formed 12 legions; then they came down through space, and Judea glowed because of their supernatural light. The shepherds who lived in the fields saw this great light, and their unforgettable song arose:

Glory to God in the Highest!
Peace on earth, goodwill towards men!

Never since then has the universe reverberated with such melodies. Indeed, angels are spiritual beings. They sing not only with their mouths but with their whole bodies, their thoughts, and their whole souls. They sing without fatigue or effort because they are full of love. Their whole beings vibrate from joy, like violins.

The angels swooped down lower and came to rest on earth itself, settling around the stable of Bethlehem. They surrounded the holy place with a fortress of beauty and harmony; a few of them even entered the barn. Jesus was resting in a manger. The shepherds and the Wise Men came and kneeled down, and the angels joined them. All the voices celebrated their gratefulness to God. Alone on the first row, the Little Angel kept quiet, his mouth tightly closed. He had decided he wouldn't sing. A simple whim? Yes, but hasn't the mouth been created to sing the praise of God? When our lips open, the glory of the Lord fills our hearts, and evil has no hold on us. But when our lips keep closed on such a beautiful day . . . and we are down on earth . . .

The devil, awaiting the slightest of our weaknesses, noticed the Little Angel who wasn't singing. He found the way to his heart and opened the Angel's eyes. He showed him the lowliness of the manger and the vulnerability of baby Jesus who looked just like any human baby. He showed him that

Mary and Joseph were poor and coarse peasants. He made the Little Angel believe that the worshipers were ridiculous in their total devotion.

"And all that attention, the music, the gifts, and the respect are for that child?" thought the Little Angel. "Of course, they are saying he is the Messiah. But he is not as handsome as I am, and also, he is hungry, he is thirsty, and he cries like small human babies. Since his birth, no one pays attention to me anymore; everyone turns towards him."

It is jealously that gave the Little Angel those ugly thoughts. He just could not rejoice about the glory of another child. He didn't want to remember anymore that the child in the manger was the Beloved Son of the Father and that all creatures in the Heavens and the earth had been created to honor him.

Christmas night was coming to an end. The angels flew back up to Heaven. And when their little friend instinctively tried to follow them, he couldn't because his wings had fallen off his shoulders. He remained alone in the night.

At dawn when the shepherds came out of the stable, they found a child, dressed in a long white robe, looking cold, and sitting in front of the door. On that morning their hearts were filled with kindness, so they covered him up and took him home with them to make a shepherd out of him. They called him Tolac, which means "little worm."

The shepherds were not rewarded for their good gesture. Tolac was handsome and very intelligent, but he scorned his adopted parents. He found them to be poor and coarse, and their work repulsed him. As soon as he became able to manage alone, he left for the big city with the intention of becoming a prince of the world.

We won't retrace the different adventures of his life. It would be a long and sad story. In fact, the older he became, the more the memories of his heavenly origins made him despise other people whom he considered inferior.

Had he only been willing to accept himself as a human being like everyone else, he was so intelligent that he could have become one of their leaders. But he felt his very race was different. All his thoughts, his words, and actions were dictated by self-adoration. He was so insatiably jealous of anything better than himself that he could not even hear of God without being scantly irritated. His pride was incensed by all efforts to glorify God.

When he became an adult, Tolac crisscrossed the seas, learned Greek, and visited Athens, Rome, and Alexandria. Because of his charm and knowledge, he made friends everywhere. His successes made him hope for better positions, but soon other people's hearts grew distant from him because he was incapable of attaching to anyone but himself. He became irritable and bitter, and when he lost his friends, he would simply move on.

Unable to win despite all he knew, Tolac threw himself into a life of corruption. He returned to Judea where his former friends were astounded by his showy, scandalous lifestyle. His house became a headquarters for dishonesty, where he taught lying and fraud to his friends. At age 35, physically worn out and filled with a growing furor against humanity, he gathered around him a few desperate companions and started a life of robbery. No traveler was spared, not even women and children. On the Sabbath he would enter a synagogue and insult God. He would beat up the rabbis, occupy the sanctuary, and steal the money that had been blessed. He was so cruel that everyone was afraid of him. Finally Tolac was caught, bound in chains, and taken to Jerusalem where the governor condemned him to be crucified.

The next day he was taken to the Hill of Calvary with two other convicts: a bandit like himself, and a Galilean patriot who had supposedly preached rebellion against Rome.

On the chest of the latter prisoner hung a cynical sign:

"The King of the Jews"

At first, Tolac felt a certain kindness toward this companion in misfortune, but soon he became disgusted by his pitiful behavior. Tolac and the other bandit marched proudly, heads high amidst the stupid crowd, while the Galilean, stumbling under his cross, cried along with the women and the children lamenting his fate.

The three men were crucified; then started the torture of atrocious thirst and the slow tearing of their flesh. The crowd jeered at the miserable "King of the Jews": "He saved others and can't save himself. If he is indeed the king of Israel, let him come down from the cross, and then we will believe in him! He trusted God, so let God deliver him now, if he loves him!"

Tolac, sneering, twisted his mouth to add

his insults to theirs, when some words loudly shouted stopped him cold: "If you are the Son of God, come down from your cross!"

"If you are the son of God . . ."? Tolac turned his head toward the Galilean. Under the crown of thorns, his eyes, the eyes of a fallen angel, immediately recognized the child of Bethlehem, the Son of God.

His heart moved with both triumph and hate. "Ah! There you are, my rival," he said to himself. "You wanted the honor of the whole world; you took away my share of that honor. You had me expelled from Paradise; you thought that all people would kneel in your presence, just like the angels did during the night of Christmas. That's what you get for pretending to be the Savior! But on earth, God does not reign. Evil does! You have been conquered. I have the satisfaction of having contributed to your defeat and, as I die, of witnessing your disgrace. Your shame is the humiliation of God himself. I am going to disappear, but I will pull you down into nothingness with me!"

Jesus turned his head and looked at the thief as if he had heard the words Tolac had thought within himself. Tolac proudly sustained Jesus' look. He was ready for a fight. He expected Jesus to react with indignation to his hate. They might exchange harsh words, but Tolac would not let himself be stared down!

Jesus, however, said nothing. His eyes were full of extreme sadness and full of extreme goodness. They seemed to say, "I also recognize you. I know who you are— the fallen angel from the night of my birth. You wanted to knock me down, and you succeeded. It's because of your jealousy and the jealousy of all human beings—it is for your crime that I am going to die!"

Strangely enough, the language of Jesus' eyes gave Tolac no opportunity for any revenge. If Jesus had become angry, Tolac would have felt he was stronger, he would have rejoiced to have lowered Jesus to his own level. He didn't expect such gentleness.

The eyes of Jesus continued to speak, "Yes, it is because of you and for you that I am dying. I could have rejected you. That's what you wanted, wasn't it? Well, no! You can't prevent me from loving you, poor fallen angel. I am winning the victory of love over you by giving my life for you."

Suddenly, the shiny, hard eyes of Tolac filled with tears. Under the eyes of Jesus, he lowered his head.

At that very moment, excited by the crowd, the other bandit started to insult Jesus. "Aren't you the Christ? Save yourself and save us!"

Tolac couldn't stand hearing others insult the one who willingly had sacrificed himself for him. Without understanding yet what was happening within him, he raised his head, opened his mouth, and, with a strong voice, started to defend his new friend. "Don't you fear God, you who are doomed to the same fate as we are?"

Having publicly acknowledged the God he had previously hated so much, Tolac suddenly felt liberated from jealousy. He immediately remembered the hymn he learned long ago for the night of Christmas:

"Glory to God in the highest!

Peace on earth, goodwill to men!"

The voice that began to sing was certainly not the pure voice of a child, nor the celestial voice of an angel. It was the hoarse voice of a man who had fallen very low and was near death.

He certainly did not sing a harmonious song, but it was a hymn, nevertheless, and a testimony to the other thief. When Tolac finished the Christmas song, he continued with the Good Friday song: "For us it is justice, because we receive what we deserve for our crimes, but this man has done nothing wrong!"

"Jesus did nothing wrong!" thought Tolac. "He was holy, and my wishing to take his place led him to his death. Ah, if only I could think of a way to free him. But it is too late. Jesus is going to die defeated, and so will I."

Tolac's eyes turned to Jesus, hoping to capture a bit of hope, but the Savior's head was leaning forward, and his eyes seemed already clouded by death. And so, as Tolac's life also faded out of his body and the shadow of death spread in his soul, his mouth acknowledged again the Redeemer. He shouted loudly, "Son of God, remember me when you come into your kingdom."

Jesus' lips hardly moved. But Tolac heard his answer clearly, "I am telling you, truly; today, you will be with me in Paradise."

At that very moment, Tolac recognized what he always knew when he was an angel, even when he had rejected God:

"Love is stronger than death. God cannot die. The one who just gave me his life will be resurrected—and through him I will also be resurrected and live again."

And Tolac let himself slip into death.

A Pillow Under One's Head

A Tale for Good Friday

*a story about being poor, about being tempted,
and about finding it hard to take a stand
if it means going against the crowd*

Two Childhood Friends

On Christmas night, when Jesus was born into this world in Bethlehem, another little boy was born in Nazareth into the home of another carpenter, the neighbor of Joseph the carpenter.

Jesus was put to sleep on straw in a manger. The other infant slept on a down pillow, made especially for him by his mother. His parents gave him the name Eliud.

The two boys grew up together and became friends. Like all children in the Middle East, they lived outside and in the fields, bringing back to their mothers armfuls of flowers, birds, and stones. Together they learned how to shepherd sheep and to whittle little reed flutes. Together they attended the synagogue school, spelling the sacred texts and reciting long segments of the law, the Psalms, and the Proverbs which they had learned by heart.

And when they became teenagers, together again they learned their fathers' craft. They practiced squaring timber, building roofs and doors, and repairing the simple tools of the Galilean peasants. They became good craftsmen.

Now they both lost their fathers when they were still very young. So Jesus and Eliud, oldest sons in large families, found themselves at the heads of their small family businesses. So they entered into partnership. They were well known for their honesty, their skills, and their precision. Everyone trusted them.

On Sabbath days, they always went to the synagogue. The other worshipers listened with respect to their commentaries on the Holy Scriptures. They were presented to other young boys as role models to be followed, because they always tried to practice God's commandments.

A Fork in the Road

When Jesus and Eliud were about 30 years old, they learned one day that John the Baptist was preaching in the desert along the River Jordan. They went to listen to him. Eliud, overcome with his need to repent, was baptized and returned to Nazareth, totally dedicated to God while he awaited the Messiah's coming.

Jesus was also baptized, and we know that he, too, heard God's calling, for as he came out of the water of the Jordan, the Holy Spirit descended upon him. But immediately he lived through enormous temptation during 40 days and 40 nights in the desert.

As soon as Jesus returned to Nazareth, Eliud began asking him questions. Jesus didn't hide anything from his friend; he explained that he was the Messiah and told him how he had fought against temptation.

The following night, as Eliud was trying to fall asleep on his down pillow, it was his turn to be tempted. Satan appeared to him disguised as an angel of light. The angel told him, "Jesus refused to work a miracle that would transform stones into bread. He was right, for people everywhere must earn their own livelihoods by hard work. Look at the farmers. They produce the bread that feeds the world from their stony, arid fields. Follow their example, and God will bless you."

Eliud listened to the tempter and decided

to devote his life to hard work.

Then the devil, still looking like an angel, told him, "Jesus refused to jump from the top of the Temple wall. He was right; he refused to impress the crowd. He chose a path which is too difficult for an ordinary person. He will always tell the truth, but, in return, people will despise him and wound him with their insults. It's better if you follow an easier path. And besides, you are not the Messiah!"

Eliud listened to the devil and resolved never to harm anyone, for fear of being harmed by them in return.

And finally, the devil said, "Jesus refused the wealth of this world which I offered him. He was right. He'll live as a poor man on this earth. I am certainly not offering you great wealth. But I am offering you enough money so that you can do a lot of good. I do not insist you dedicate your life to me. You already dedicated it to God, and you did the right thing. You will only have to acknowledge me with a small daily nod. The rest of the time, you will belong to your friend Jesus."

Eliud listened to the devil. What he heard brought peace to his soul, and he fell asleep on his down pillow.

Indecision

A few days later, Jesus left his family and headed for Capernaum where he started teaching. While he was away, Eliud took care of their little carpentry business. Since Eliud was a hard worker and a good businessman, the business grew. He hired workmen and traveled from one building site to another to supervise the projects.

Eliud respected the law, and so he always stopped all work on the Sabbath in order to serve God. As he came out of the synagogue, he gave away large gifts of money. On the street when prayer time came, he was not afraid to stop walking, standing motionless for a long time. Many people greeted him on the public square, and he enjoyed these honors greatly.

He often heard from Jesus and was impressed by his successes. "We are both blessed by God," he thought. "We are privileged. We must thank the Lord."

One Sabbath day, Jesus returned to his hometown. Crowds of people went to the synagogue to hear this speaker from their own village who had become so well-known.

Very proudly, Eliud sat on the front row, his usual place. Everyone expected Jesus to pronounce words of grace and encouragement. He began by reading a passage from Isaiah about the Messiah: "The Spirit of the Lord is upon me." Then he declared, "Today, his word is accomplished." Nothing could have been more disagreeable for his former schoolmates and playmates to hear. "How so?" they murmured, pushing each other with their elbows. "He is the son of common people, and he pretends to pose as the Messiah!"

Eliud felt very restless and embarrassed on his bench. Deep in his heart he knew Jesus was right. He felt like standing up, turning around to face his friends, and repeating again Jesus' speech. He wanted to round off the sharp edges a bit, but then make the audience understand that he, Eliud, Jesus' best friend, could confirm that Jesus had truly been selected by God.

Meanwhile, Jesus could feel the opposition against him, yet he continued to speak in progressively sharper words: "It is only in his homeland that a prophet is despised," he exclaimed. "Despised by his own relatives and his own home." Oh, how clumsy of him! thought Eliud. He could say the same things with a little more tact.

In the back of the synagogue, anger was rumbling. When Jesus compared himself to the prophet Elijah, who was taken in by a widow he didn't know when he was forced to flee his homeland, some young men moved forward to grab him. The religious service finally exploded into great confusion.

Eliud jumped to his feet and raised one arm. A single word from him could have quieted the crowd. But his speech remained stuck in his throat. He tried to commandeer the situation: "Stop! Don't lay hands upon the one chosen by the Lord!" But nothing came out. He was paralyzed by the possible consequences. He could picture himself losing his reputation, ruined, fleeing with Jesus, condemned to adventures he feared.

His arm fell back to his side, and the young men dragged Jesus to a mountaintop above the city. They wanted to throw him off a cliff.

Eliud did not run after them. Horror-stricken, incapable of thinking, he went back home to pray.

As dusk came, he heard a knock on the door. It was Jesus. He had a head wound; his clothes were torn, but he was alive. Eliud took him in his arms, thanking the Lord that he hadn't been killed. He dressed Jesus' wounds and gave him new clothes. Eliud didn't know which made him happier—was it the release of his friend or his own relief? If Jesus had died, he would have felt responsible. But Jesus was safe and sound. And Eliud felt innocent!

Full of enthusiasm, he exclaimed, "Master, I'll follow you wherever you go!"

Jesus stopped him with a hand gesture. "Eliud," he said, "the foxes have their dens and the birds in the sky have their nests, but the Son of Man has no place to rest his head."

The Messiah helped himself to some food. And as he opened the door to continue on his ministry, Eliud saw the dark night and felt the cold air. He gave a long look at his comfortable room. "It is settled," he said to Jesus. "I'll catch up with you . . . tomorrow."

But the next day, after sleeping deeply on his down pillow, Eliud did some thinking. Before leaving, shouldn't he straighten out all his businesses so that his young brother would find everything in good order?

One week later, he was still at home.

Separation

Eliud's conscience was definitely relieved—and why? He was told that Jesus' talks were becoming more and more extravagant—"Whoever wants to become my disciple must hate his father, his mother, his family, his house!"

Jesus' mother, Mary, was totally upset. His brothers were humiliated along with their mother. They decided to find their crazy brother and bring him home. It was time to stop the scandals everyone was talking about.

Two days later, Eliud saw the brothers come home. "Do you know the affront our mother received?" they said. "When we tried to talk to Jesus, he pointed to a collection of toll-gatherers, beggars, and prostitutes who were following him. 'These are my mother and brothers,' he exclaimed!"

Eliud congratulated himself for not having followed Jesus. Jesus' fame has led him astray, he mused. He doesn't respect the Lord's command anymore to honor one's father and mother!

About that time, Eliud suddenly decided to marry a beautiful young woman in the village. He had been resisting a strong and persistent desire to have her, because he sensed she was a superficial person who would demand the focus of his life. But now, to honor his fiancé, he built a house on the edge of town with his own hands. It was the most beautiful, the whitest, of all the houses in Nazareth. The people approved of it. "It is his right," they said, "since he is a builder."

Eliud's marriage ceremony turned out to be a moving religious event. He invited Jesus to come, but he asked to be excused because he was so engrossed with ministering among the poor. Eliud was offended.

Eliud's wife turned out to be a talented and thrifty homemaker. She wove beautiful outfits for her husband. She prevented him from overworking. In turn, Eliud had extra time which he devoted to studying the Scriptures.

ANGELS AND DONKEYS

He became a very important man in the village. In fact, he became doubly devout in order to cover over some of his business practices. He was admired for the way he commented on the holy books. He could discuss with the doctors of the law as though he were one of them. He came to be known as a learned teacher. But all of that activity did not prevent his wealth from growing from one month to the other.

Yet in his heart he hid a deep melancholy. He began lying on his bed without speaking and refusing all the food his wife brought him. She couldn't understand what was happening.

"Can you imagine," she said to Mary, her neighbor, "he, who is the best of husbands and the fairest of bosses, he who scrupulously practices all of God's commands, he is full of remorse! He reproaches himself for not having followed Jesus, the fanatic preacher!"

One morning Eliud could not stand it anymore. He left the house very early without wakening his wife so he could catch up with Jesus.

"Good Master," he exclaimed, falling on his knees, "tell me what I must do to receive eternal life."

Jesus knew Eliud. He never expected more of him than he could actually give—great honesty, sincere friendship, and not much courage.

"You know the commandments," Jesus answered. "Just put them into practice."

"But, you know," replied Eliud emphatically, "that I did just that, ever since we were children together."

Jesus looked at him and felt deep love for his old friend. Shouldn't he be helped to salvation like so many others? Shouldn't he also receive the joy of the Kingdom?

"If you want to be perfect," said Jesus, "go sell everything you own and give it to the poor. Then come and follow me."

Eliud looked at Jesus with the eyes of a lost person. He saw the feet of this prophet, bruised by the stones on the roads, his clothes worn out like those of a pauper, his tired expression. He thought of his own wife, his mother, his house, and the workers who depended on him for their salaries. He stood up without a word, and with his head bent low, he left. Barely thinking about what he was doing, he walked back to Nazareth.

A few weeks later he heard, with some satisfaction, the rumor that Jesus was now attacking the Holy Law of Moses in his speeches—washing practices, the Sabbath, fasting. People even reported that he attacked the doctors of the law, the Pharisees, and the local leaders!

Eliud was personally offended. He felt this was blasphemy against God himself. He felt pressed to stand up and defend the established order. From then on, when he spoke in the synagogue on the Sabbath, he often made unkind allusions about the fallen Messiah. In fact, he used the scriptures to discourse against Jesus.

It was the only way he could stifle the protests of his own conscience.

Good Intentions

Amazing events began happening, and at a faster and faster pace. Back from the Passover celebration, some Galilean travelers described how Jesus, claiming he was the Messiah, had entered Jerusalem triumphantly, leading a large procession. His preaching at the Temple was met by fiery opposition from the priests. They threatened to arrest him, so he had to hide every night in Bethany.

On Thursday evening while Jesus appeared in front of the Sanhedrin (the Jewish Supreme Council), Eliud tossed back and forth on his bed, unable to sleep. He could imagine Jesus looking as he had when he stood in the door frame the evening of his Nazareth speech, pale, dressed in torn clothes, a wound on his head. Jesus was telling him, "Eliud, my friend, I am alone. They have abandoned me. All of them. Will you not come help me?"

The next day he tried to forget his nightmare, but in vain. Eliud kept telling himself that, as before, Jesus would escape from the hands of his tormentors. But as night came closer, he gathered all the money he had on hand, telling his wife, "Tomorrow I will leave for Jerusalem to free my friend, unless he has already been arrested!" He was deciding to attempt anything, even the impossible, to save Jesus.

Strengthened by his decision, he stretched out on his bed for a few hours of rest, intending to get on his way very early the next morning.

But when he woke up, the sun was already high. And he learned that some terrible news had come to his town. The previous day at 3 o'clock, Jesus had died; he had been crucified. He could rest his head, crowned with thorns, against only a wooden pillow during his agony.

Eliud went home without a word. Cowardice, fearing other people's opinion, loving wealth, the allure of honor, indecision, pride, laziness—all those crimes roared up against him, accusing him. He pushed away his pillow and his colorful blankets. He tore his clothing and covered his head with ashes, for he wanted to mourn Jesus, as well as his own conscience. His wife could hear him crying loudly, but she didn't dare go near him. Around noon when he had calmed down a bit, she came to him with a tray full of his favorite dishes. "Get up," she said. "Eat!"

But he refused to be consoled by her, so she took him in her arms and whispered in his ear, "Come on! Take hold of yourself! It is clear Jesus has made a mistake. Had he been the Messiah, he wouldn't have died. He would have triumphed over his enemies. But he attacked the law of God itself, and God punished him."

"He was my friend," answered Eliud, "and I had promised to follow him."

"But he was crazy!" continued his wife. "A very seductive madman, that is true, but a madman nevertheless! God prevented you from following him several times. Look where he is now, while you, you are prosperous! Can't you see divine blessings in the success of all your undertakings?"

His eyes still filled with tears, Eliud sat up and took a bit of food. It gave him pleasure since the dish was very good, and he finished the whole thing. He looked at his wife with a smile full of sadness and thankfulness. She rejoiced to see him becoming reasonable again, and she straightened out his bed.

"Be sure to rest!" she said as she left the room.

Eliud fell into a deep sleep, his head nestled on his down pillow.

In the tomb of Joseph, the head of Jesus rested on a stone.

The Sword

a story about Christian nonviolence,
which Pastors Trocmé and Theis
espoused in the area's struggle
with the Nazi persecutions

On the sixth day of the week, exactly a week after Jesus was arrested in the garden of Gethsemane, a middle-aged man with a square beard and a bald head knocked on the door of Chomer, the garden's elderly caretaker.

"Old man," he said, "isn't this the garden of Gethsemane? I fear I've lost my way. The other evening it was full of rocks and thorny bushes, and this morning I find it all clean and well tilled."

"Yes," answered Chomer, "you are indeed at the garden of the olive trees. What can I do for you?"

"Well, here is the story," said the man with some hesitation. "During the riot that took place here, I lost a sword. Did you find it?"

He was still speaking when a youngster arrived out of breath. "Caretaker, caretaker!" said the boy. "Didn't you. . .didn't you find a sword I picked up the other night after the fight? I had hidden it in a bush."

He was still speaking when a handsome woman, walking straight in spite of her age, appeared and said, "Old man, you must have found a sword in this garden. You must hand it to me!"

In spite of having a rounded back and hands full of calluses, the gardener had a face with the expression of a great nobleman. He invited them all in, sat them around his table, served them bread and honey, and told them,

"It is true. I did find a sword after a large crowd armed with swords and sticks entered my garden and trampled all my promising plants. But I cannot give this sword to anyone except the one who will contribute to the good of Israel's people."

The bald man with the square beard spoke first. "Well," he said, "here is my idea. I came to fetch this sword so that I could put it back where it belongs. I am simply following orders from my master Jesus, the prophet of Nazareth arrested here the other evening. Early last week I discovered that the leaders of the priests wanted to put him to death. So I sneaked into the Temple to steal this sword which was hanging near the altar of perfumes. When the policemen came to grab Jesus in the garden, I was ready to defend him. I hit the High Priest with the sword and cut off his ear.

"But, you see, my master didn't like what I did. He cured my victim and then told me sternly, 'All those who take the sword will perish by the sword. Put the sword back in its place.' I was so terrorized that, instead of obeying Jesus, I threw away my sword and ran off in the night. As you know, Jesus was crucified the next day. I am guilty. It is because of the sword that he was accused as an evil-doer.

"This morning I escaped from the watchful eye of the High Priest's police. I have come to repair my mistake. As Jesus ordered, I came to get the sword and return it to the Temple, next to the altar of perfumes. This is how I can serve my people. When he returns, the Messiah must find the sword in its place for he will need it to exterminate the enemies of his kingdom."

The old caretaker turned to the young boy who was growing impatient. "And you," he said, "what do you have to tell?"

"I don't like the way Simon Peter who is present here behaved," he started. "The other evening after the Prophet was arrested, Simon Peter cowardly threw his sword away.

And along with the other disciples, he abandoned the one person he should have defended to the end. He ran away in the night. So I picked up the sword and hid it in a bush. And you, caretaker, you are going to give it to me, because today I am leaving with other patriots. In the caves near the Dead Sea, we are forming a militia to save the Messiah who is coming back. Jesus himself declared that the Son of Man would bring the sword, not peace. That's why when he returns, he must find a large army to serve him. That way it won't be hard to kick the Romans out and re-establish David's kingdom. This is how I'll serve Israel, my people."

"Hush!" interrupted the woman, "stop, young man! I cannot stand your words! This sword has already done too much harm, and it should be prevented from doing more harm. I am the mother of Jesus of Nazareth whom the leaders of the priests arrested here the other evening and then had him crucified by Pilate. Thirty years ago, when I came to present my little boy at the temple, the old man Simeon received him in his arms. He turned toward me and said, 'A sword will pierce your soul.' At that time I did not understand the meaning of those words. It was only last Friday, a week ago, that I grasped their meaning. Oh, how it hurt! There was my son, dying as a criminal between two criminals. It's because of that cursed sword which you raised to defend him, Simon Peter. Yet you knew well that Jesus, my son, did not want to answer evil with evil."

Turning to the caretaker, the woman begged him, "Give me the sword. It is a sword burdened with scandal. Give it to me! I want to take it back to Galilee. And when I reach the shores of Lake Genesareth, I will tie a stone to its handle and throw it to the bottom of the water. Then it will never pierce the souls of other mothers. This is the way I will serve Israel, my people."

There was silence in the little hut, and then Chomer started to speak. "It is my turn to tell you my story. I'm going to tell you a secret. I have not always been the poor gardener you see in front of you. Thirty years ago, I was the chief of King Herod's body of guards. As you remember, Herod had set out to return David's kingdom to its historical borders. He even succeeded, thanks to his alliance with the Romans. Then he began rebuilding the Temple, and he dotted the country with sumptuous palaces. He relentlessly fought the enemies of our people and pursued the agitators who could have created trouble within his kingdom. I was a young patriot, waiting for the return of the kingdom of Israel and the coming of the Messiah. That is why I entered the service of this king; I saw him as a forerunner of the Messiah.

"Well, Herod noticed my zeal and summoned me to his throne. He announced, 'I appoint you chief of my guards. You will go to the Temple in Jerusalem; there you will take the sword located near the altar of perfumes off its hook. It is the sword of Judas Maccabeus, the hero of our national independence who purified the Temple after getting rid of our enemies. Unfortunately, Judas was killed in the Beerzet battle, but they found his sword on the battlefield and hung it inside the Temple in memory of him. An old tradition says that the one who will use it will prepare for the coming of the Messiah. You are the one designated to accomplish this mission. Go, take this sword, and be my servant.'

"I was a soldier and so I obeyed King Herod. I was young, and the idea of a glorious career filled me with impatience and enthusiasm. Judas Maccabeus' sword was a magnificent weapon—heavier and longer than an ordinary sword. I was tall, strong, and full of ambition in those days. I carried it, hoping some day to become the liberator of my people, just like Judas Maccabeus. However, I soon learned that by taking the sword off its hook, I was adding one more horror to Herod's numerous horrors. To this last horror I would soon add an unforgivable crime.

"Listen, Simon Peter. Last Friday when I found this glorious and cursed sword in my garden, I immediately recognized it. I got scared. How had this weapon of evil omen come back to me? I was sure that it had once more brought suffering and evil. I know now it was a very great evil, indeed, since the Prophet of Nazareth isn't among us anymore."

There was a new silence in the hut. Then the gardener continued in a softer voice, as if he were making a confession, "Listen now to the rest of my tragic story. After I was appointed chief of the guards, King Herod informed me that a threatening rebellion had exploded in Bethlehem. He ordered us to exterminate all the newborn male infants in town. I felt overwhelmed with unspeakable horror. But as a military man, I had to obey the orders of my chief, so that is what I did. The morning after this terrible night, I mechanically wiped Judas Maccabeus' sword, trying to purify it of all the innocent blood soiling it. Some shepherds ran towards me from the neighboring fields. They surrounded me, threatening me. I was so overwhelmed with shame I could hardly stand their shouting at me: 'What have you done! Not only did you slaughter our beloved children, but you also killed the newly born Messiah! We saw angels and bowed completely in front of him. He was in that stable over there, the one that is now only smoking ashes after your damaging march through here. And it is you, a Jew, who actually did that? Get away from here, you cursed man!'

"So I ran away towards Jerusalem, just like a cursed man! I sent in my resignation to Herod, and I put the sword back on its hook in the Temple, where it should have stayed and where you took it from, Simon Peter. Since that day, and of my own free will, I have led a life of repentance and poverty in this garden. Old age has come. Will God forgive me my crime? I who wanted to prepare the arrival of the Messiah, I was the cause of his death because of this cursed sword. So listen to me, my friends. Be aware that the person who wants to serve the God of love with violent means is, in truth, the enemy of God and of the people of Israel."

Silence weighed heavily on the gardener and his three visitors. It was a silence full of remorse and grief. Tightening his fists, the young boy stood crying with tears of anger and resentment. The old caretaker avoided his visitors' eyes.

That's when Mary looked at Simon Peter in a strange, almost relaxed way. She smiled slightly as she asked him, "Should we tell him the whole truth?" Simon nodded. Then Mary walked over to the old man and put her hand on his shoulder. "Raise your head," she said. "I have great news for you. It is still a secret, but soon the whole world will hear about

Jesus of Nazareth, my son. He was arrested the other evening in this garden. He was crucified and he died. And he was the Messiah chosen by God to liberate not only his people, the people of Israel, but all the children of God scattered over the earth. This Jesus who died was raised back to life by God during the morning of the first day of this week. I met my son who is alive again, and we ate and drank with his disciples."

"Woman," answered Chomer without even lifting his head, "you are wrong. The prophet of Nazareth cannot be the Messiah, for the Messiah was born in Bethlehem 30 years ago, and I am the one who killed him then with my own hands."

"God works great miracles," said Mary. "You did not kill the Messiah of Bethlehem 30 years ago, because the child and I—his mother—we had left the city a few minutes before your arrival."

The old man stood up, almost shouting, "Woman, what are you saying?"

"I am telling you, you did not kill my son Jesus the Messiah. I am his mother, and I brought him into the world 30 years ago in a stable in Bethlehem. While you and your men were hurrying to carry out Herod's cruel orders, an angel sent by the Lord appeared in my husband Joseph's dreams saying, 'Get up, take the little child and his mother. Flee to Egypt and stay there until I speak to you again, for Herod is looking for this child to kill him.' So in the middle of the night, Joseph picked up the child, and we fled to Egypt before you got here. Old man, God is so powerful and so good that he repairs even the unrepairable crimes we commit. You thought you killed the Messiah, but through his grace, God transformed your crime into deliverance. Simon Peter also swung the sword, causing the death of Jesus, just as you believed you did. But by bringing Jesus back to life, God transformed my son's death into salvation for Simon Peter, and for everyone who repents and believes. Do you believe that? And now, give me the sword, for Jesus is alive again. He does not need to be protected. Get rid of the sword forever so we don't risk spreading murder and crime at the hands of insane people."

The old man stood up, staggering a bit like someone just freed from a crushing weight. "Well," he exclaimed, "I also want to share with you some news which will bring you great joy. The sword has already disappeared. God guided my hand. Stand up and come to see."

He opened a door to the shed where he kept his gardening tools. On the ground was a plow, its plowshare brand new.

"Look at this plowshare," said the old man. "See how shiny it is! The ground of Gethsemane is full of stones. I could not till it anymore with my old wooden plow. The other morning, as soon as I found the sword of Judas Maccabeus in a bush, I walked up to the Temple to ask God what I should do with it. As I was praying, I recalled Isaiah's old prophecy, 'Come, let us climb the mountain of the Lord. . . for from Zion will come the Law, and from Jerusalem the Word of the Lord. He will be the judge of nations, the arbitrator of numerous peoples. . .No nation will draw the sword against another anymore, and no one will learn war anymore. . . From their swords, they will forge plowshares.'

"Here, I thought, is the Lord's answer! So I took the sword to Tubalcain the blacksmith for him to make a plowshare for my plow. And since Monday night I have tilled the earth of Gethsemane. I pulled stones and thorns out of it. I threw new seeds on the ground. A few weeks from now a harvest will ripen on the very same spot where the Messiah was handed over to wicked men. And now Simon Peter, John Mark, and Mary. Go tell the Messiah, since he is alive, that I would like to welcome him in my house. To him alone I shall return the sword of Judas Maccabeus which has been forever transformed into an instrument of peace."

About the Author

André Trocmé was an ordained minister in the French Reformed Church. He spent the World War II years in Le Chambon-sur-Lignon, France. After working for several years for the European Fellowship of Reconciliation, he returned to the parish ministry in Geneva, Switzerland. He always remained on the fringes of the established French Protestant church because of his pacifist beliefs.

About the Translator

Nelly Trocmé Hewett first came to the United States as an au pair girl and remained as a college student. She raised her three children in Minneapolis where she taught French in prep schools. She is presently retired in St. Paul, Minnesota.

ANGELS AND DONKEYS